Whose dark or troubled mind will you step into next? Detective or assassin, victim or accomplice? Can you tell reality from delusion, truth from deception, when you're spinning in the whirl of a thriller or trapped in the grip of an unsolvable mystery? You can't trust your senses and you can't trust anyone: you're in the hands of the undisputed masters of crime fiction.

Writers of some of the greatest thrillers and mysteries on earth, who inspired those who followed. Writers whose talents range far and wide—a mathematics genius, a cultural icon, a master of enigma, a legendary dream team. Their books are found on shelves in houses throughout their home countries—from Asia to Europe, and everywhere in between. Timeless books that have been devoured, adored and handed down through the decades. Iconic books that have inspired films, and demand to be read and read again.

So step inside a dizzying world of criminal masterminds with **Pushkin Vertigo**. The only trouble you might have is leaving them behind.

PUSHKIN VERTIGO

Pushkin Vertigo
71–75 Shelton Street
London, WC2H 9JQ

Original Text © by Éditions Denoël,
1954 (*D'entre les morts*)

Translation by Geoffrey Sainsbury

First published by Pushkin Vertigo in 2015

0 0 1

ISBN 978 1 782270 80 5

Text designed and typeset by Tetragon, London
Printed and bound by
CPI Group (UK) Ltd, Croydon CR0 4YY

www.pushkinpress.com

PART
ONE

ONE

'Look here!' said Gévigne. 'I want you to keep an eye on my wife.'

'The devil!… Running off the rails, is she?'

'Not in the way you think.'

'What's the matter, then?'

'It isn't easy to explain. She's queer… I'm worried about her.'

'What are you afraid of, exactly?'

Gévigne hesitated. He looked at Flavières, and the latter could see very well what was holding him back: Gévigne wasn't sure how much trust he could place in his friend.

Basically he was much the same as Flavières had known him fifteen years earlier at the *Faculté de Droit*—friendly and expansive on the surface, but just the reverse underneath, shy, unhappy, turned in upon himself. It was all very well to burst in with open arms, exclaiming:

'Roger, old boy!… It's mighty good to see you again.'

Flavières had seen at once that the cordiality was slightly put on, as though the scene had been rehearsed beforehand and then just a little overplayed. Gévigne was fidgety, his laugh too loud. Not much. Oh no! If the note was wrong, it was only by a fraction of a semi-tone, yet Flavières could feel instinctively that the other was not altogether at ease. He wanted at a blow to wipe out the fifteen years that had passed, years which had changed them both physically. Gévigne was almost completely bald and his chin had lost its clean line. His eyebrows had turned rusty in colour, and there were now freckles at the side of his nose. As for Flavières, he was not only thinner, but, since his trouble, had acquired a stoop. And his hands went clammy at the thought that Gévigne might ask him why he was now practising as a lawyer, considering that he had studied law to go into the police.

'I'm not exactly afraid of anything,' answered Gévigne.

He held out a handsome case full of cigars. His clothes too bespoke wealth, and rings glittered on his fingers as he tore off a little pink match from a book of matches bearing the name of a smart restaurant. He hollowed his cheeks before slowly blowing out a cloud of smoke.

'It's really a question of atmosphere,' he said.

Yes, he had changed a lot. He had tasted power. One could see in him the man who took the chair at board meetings and had useful contacts in high places. Yet, with all that, his eyes were always on the move and only too ready to take refuge beneath those heavy drooping eyelids.

'Atmosphere?' asked Flavières, with just a touch of irony.

'I think it's the right word,' Gévigne insisted. 'My wife is perfectly happy. We've been married four years, or will have been in two months' time. We have everything we want; my factory at Le Havre has been working at full blast ever since the mobilization, which is, incidentally, the reason why I haven't been called up. So you see: under the circumstances we can count ourselves fortunate.'

'Children?' put in Flavières.

'No.'

'Go on.'

'I was saying that Madeleine had everything to make a woman

happy. And yet there's something wrong. She has always had a rather strange character, a bit unstable—up one moment, down the next—but in the last few months she has become rapidly worse.'

'You've seen a doctor, I suppose?'

'Of course. Several. The very best. And there's nothing the matter with her, nothing whatever.'

'Physically, you mean—but psychologically?'

'Nothing on that side either. At least…'

He fidgeted with his hands, and brushed away some ash that had fallen on his waistcoat.

'There is something all the same. I tell you, it's quite a case. At first I too thought there was something at the back of her mind troubling her—some unreasoning fear provoked by the war, for instance. She would suddenly relapse into silence and hardly hear what was said to her. Or she would stare at something—and I can't tell you what a queer impression it made. I know this sounds absurd, but it was as though she was seeing things invisible to the rest of us… Then, when she came back to her normal self, she would have a slightly bewildered expression on her face, as though it took her a little time to recognize her surroundings, and even her own husband…'

He relit the cigar, which he had allowed to go out. And he too stared vacantly in front of him with that baffled air that Flavières knew of old.

'If she's not ill, physically or mentally,' said Flavières with a touch of asperity, 'she's putting on an act. She's probably—'

Gévigne raised his hand to stop him.

'I thought of that, and I've been watching her discreetly. One day I followed her… She went into the Bois de Boulogne, sat down in front of the lake, and stayed there without moving, contemplating the water.'

'There's nothing in that.'

'Oh yes there is… though it's not so easy to explain. She was looking at the water with a quite extraordinary gravity and attention, as though it was of the utmost importance to her… And then, that evening, she blandly told me she hadn't been out of the house. Of course, I didn't let on that I'd seen her.'

Flavières kept on finding, then losing again, the fellow-student he had known, and the game was getting on his nerves.

'Listen,' he said. 'Either your wife's ill or she's up to some game or other. There's no getting away from that. And, if it's the latter, there's probably a man in the background.'

Gévigne stretched his hand out towards the ash-tray on the desk and with a flick of his finger knocked off a long cylinder of white ash. He smiled sadly.

'Your mind works exactly as mine did. But I'm absolutely certain Madeleine is not an unfaithful wife. On the other hand, Professor Lavarenne assures me she's absolutely normal. For the rest, why should she put on an act, as you call it? To gain what? After all, one doesn't build up a mountain of make-believe just for fun. One doesn't go and study the water in the Bois for two hours for nothing. And it isn't as if that was an isolated instance. There have been plenty of others.'

'Have you tried to have it out with her?'

'Yes, naturally… I've asked her what it was took hold of her when she suddenly went off into a dream.'

'What did she say?'

'That I oughtn't to bother about it; that she didn't dream; that she worried like anyone else about the present state of the world.'

'Was she annoyed you asked her?'

'Yes, a bit. But still more embarrassed.'

'Did you get the impression she was lying?'

'Not at all. The impression I got was that she was afraid… Look here: do you remember—this'll make you smile—a German film called *Jacob Boehme* we saw at the *Ursulines* back in the 'twenties?'

'Yes.'

'Do you remember the expression on the mystic's face when he was caught in a sort of visionary trance? And he tried to find excuses and hide the fact that he had visions… Well, Madeleine's face looked like that German actor's. A bewildered, groping look; I might almost say a drunken look.'

'Come on! You're not trying to tell me your wife has visions, are you?'

'I knew that would be your reaction—just as it was mine. For a long time I held out, refusing to believe what I saw.'

'Does she go to church?'

'Like hundreds of others—because it's the thing to do.'

'Has she ever dabbled in fortune-telling or any of that psychic stuff?'

'Never. She's never taken up anything of that sort. This is quite different. Something seems to happen to her, and all of a sudden you realize she's somewhere else.'

'Do you think it's quite involuntary?'

'I'm sure of it. I've been watching her long enough now to know something about it. She feels the attack coming and she tries to ward it off, by talking or busying herself with something, by switching on the wireless. Sometimes she goes to the window and opens it as though she needed a breath of air... If, at that moment, I come to the rescue, if I start joking or chatting of this or that, it seems to give her something to hold on to and she's able to keep on this side of the line... I'm sorry to be so long-winded, but it isn't easy to make her condition intelligible to anyone else... If, on the other hand, I pretend to be absorbed in my own thoughts, then over she goes—it never fails. She seems to go rigid and her eyes seem to be intently watching something which moves—at least I suppose it moves, since her eyes do—she heaves a sigh and passes the back of her hand across her forehead. Then for five minutes, ten perhaps, but rarely more, she's for all the world like a sleep-walker.'

'Are her movements jerky?'

'No... At least... It's difficult to say... As a matter of fact I've never seen anyone walk in his sleep... But you don't really get the impression she's asleep. She's absent-minded, as though her body no longer belonged to her, as though she had become someone else. Oh, I know it's ridiculous, but I can't put it better than that: *she's someone else.*'

Gévigne's eyes were genuinely troubled.

'Someone else!' growled Flavières. 'That doesn't mean anything.'

'You don't believe there can be certain... certain influences which...?'

But Gévigne gave it up. He put his cigar down on the edge of the ash-tray and wrung his hands.

'Since I've begun,' he went on presently, 'I'd better get it all off my chest... Among Madeleine's ancestors was a strange woman whose name was Pauline Lagerlac. She was a great-grandmother. Not so very far away, you see... When she was thirteen or fourteen she had a rather mysterious illness—I really don't know how to explain it—she had queer convulsions, and people heard strange sounds coming from her room...'

'Tappings on the wall?'

'Yes.'

'Scraping noises, as though furniture was being moved?'

'Yes.'

'I know. They're symptoms often found in girls of that age, though I don't believe anybody's ever found an explanation for them. They generally don't last long.'

'I'm not very well up myself in these matters,' went on Gévigne, 'but it seems fairly certain that Pauline Lagerlac remained all her life a bit odd. She wanted to become a nun, then gave up the idea. Finally she married; then, after a few years, committed suicide... for no reason at all.'

'What age was she then?'

Gévigne took out his handkerchief and dabbed his mouth.

'Twenty-five,' he murmured. 'Madeleine's age now.'

'The devil!'

The two men were silent. Flavières turned the story over in his mind. Then he asked:

'Your wife knows, I suppose?... About Pauline Lagerlac?'

'As a matter of fact she doesn't... I got the story from my mother-in-law. She told me soon after our marriage. At the time I didn't attach any importance to it, listening merely out of politeness... If I had known then!... My mother-in-law's dead now, and there's no one I can turn to for any further information.'

'When she told you, do you think she had any idea at the back of her mind?'

'I don't think so. The subject cropped up quite accidentally.

Only, I remember clearly her saying I was on no account to tell Madeleine. She wasn't at all proud herself of having a person of doubtful sanity in the family and thought it better her daughter shouldn't know.'

'You say this Pauline Lagerlac killed herself for no reason at all... That doesn't sound very likely.'

'There was no reason that anyone could find out. She seemed happy. She had given birth to a son a few months before, and everybody expected that to be a stabilizing influence. And then, suddenly, one day—'

'Still, I don't see how this has anything to do with your wife.'

'You will,' said Gévigne with a heavy sigh. 'You will... When her mother died, she naturally inherited a lot of family things, including some jewellery and ornaments that had come down from her great-grandmother, among them an amber necklace. And these beads seem to have a special meaning for her. She's always fiddling with them and gazing at them with... with a sort of nostalgia. And we've got a portrait of Pauline Lagerlac at home, painted by herself—for, like Madeleine, she was an amateur painter. Madeleine has spent hours staring at that picture, as though fascinated. More than that: I once caught her with the picture propped up beside a mirror—she had the amber necklace on and was trying to do her hair like the woman in the portrait...'

With obvious embarrassment, Gévigne went on:

'She's done it like that ever since—with a heavy bun on her neck.'

'Is there any resemblance between her and her great-grandmother?'

'A little perhaps... a very vague one.'

'To come back to my first question: what are you afraid of, exactly?'

Gévigne picked up his cigar and studied it gloomily.

'I hardly like to tell you… One thing's certain: Madeleine's no longer the same… And… and I can't help thinking sometimes—'

'What?'

'That the woman living with me isn't Madeleine.'

Flavières got up from his chair with a strained laugh.

'Come on! If it isn't your wife, who is it? Pauline Lagerlac?… My dear Paul, you're letting your mind run off the rails… Have a drink. Port? Cinzano? Cap Corse?'

'Port.'

As Flavières went into the dining-room for a tray and some glasses, Gévigne called after him:

'And what about you? I haven't even asked you if you were married?'

'No,' answered Flavières dully, 'and I've no desire to be.'

'It was only by chance I heard you'd left the police.'

Silence in the dining-room.

'Can I give you a hand?'

Gévigne hoisted himself out of his armchair and went to the door leading to the next room. Flavières was uncorking a bottle. Gévigne leant against the door-post.

'Nice place you've got… Sorry to be bothering you with my troubles… Mighty glad to see you again… I ought to have rung you up before coming, but I live in such a rush these days…'

Flavières straightened himself and calmly took the cork off the corkscrew. The difficult moment was over.

'You said you were building ships now, didn't you?' he asked, filling two glasses.

'Small craft. But it's a very big contract… At the Ministry they seem to be expecting some hard knocks…'

'I should think they are! We can't go on with this phony war for ever. And we'll soon be in May… Well, here's luck, Paul.'

'All the best, Roger.'

They looked into each other's eyes as they lifted their glasses. Standing up, Gévigne was short and square. The light from the window fell full on to his Roman features, fleshy ears, and truly noble forehead. Not that Gévigne had anything great in him: a little Provençal blood in his veins had sufficed to endow him with this deceptive profile of a proconsul. This war was going to make the fellow a millionaire… Flavières banished the thought, ashamed of it. Was he not himself profiting from the absence of others who had been called up? It is true he had failed to pass a medical, but was that really a valid excuse? He put his glass back on the tray.

'I can see this business of yours is going to get under my skin… Has your wife anyone at the front she might be worried about?'

'A few distant cousins we never see… No one she really cares about.'

'How did you meet her?'

'Accidentally. It was quite romantic.'

Gévigne studied his glass. He was weighing his words. Always that fear of making himself ridiculous which had paralysed him as a student, making him fail in his *vivas*.

'I met her in Rome, where I was doing some business. We were staying in the same hotel.'

'Which one?'

'The *Continental*.'

'What was she doing in Rome?'

'Studying painting. She had a real talent, or that's what they say. I'm not much of a judge of that sort of thing.'

'Was she studying with a view to teaching?'

'Good heavens, no!… Just because she liked it. She never had to think about earning her living. Why, she had her own car at the age of eighteen. Her father was a big industrialist.'

Gévigne turned and walked back into the office. In the way he walked, at any rate, he showed real assurance now. Formerly he had had a hesitant step, a sort of stammer in his movements. His wife's money had transformed him.

'Does she still paint?'

'No. She gave it up little by little. Found she hadn't got the time. The life they lead, these Parisian women!'

'But… these troubles you've been telling me about… they must have had a cause. Can't you think of any incident that might have started the ball rolling? A quarrel, for instance, or a bit of bad news… You must have thought of that.'

'Of course I've thought of it, and I've racked my brains to discover something… Don't forget I spend half the week at Le Havre.'

'These… these attacks, as you call them… could they have anything to do with your being away?'

'I don't think so… The first one occurred soon after I got back. It was a Saturday. I had found her in excellent spirits; then in the evening I thought there was something odd about her. Naturally I didn't pay much attention to it at that moment, particularly as I was tired at the end of a heavy week.'

'Before that?'

'She may have been a bit moody at times, but no more than anybody is.'

'On that Saturday, you're sure nothing unusual happened?'

'Absolutely. All the more so as we were together the whole time. I got back about ten in the morning. Madeleine had just got up. We chatted for a while... But you can't expect me to remember every detail of the day. There was no reason for me to remember them. I know we lunched at home.'

'Where do you live?'

Gévigne looked surprised, then smiled.

'Of course... I was forgetting we've completely lost touch with each other. I bought a block of flats on the Avenue Kléber, quite close to the Etoile. We live in one of them. Here—you'd better have my card.'

'Thanks.'

'In the afternoon we went out. I had to drop in at the Ministry for a few minutes, but she wasn't left alone for long. After that we pottered about round the Opera, and then... Well, it was an afternoon like any other.'

'And the attack?'

'It came on just after supper.'

'Can you give me the exact date?'

'Really! How should I know?'

But he studied the calendar on the lawyer's desk.

'I know it was in February, and towards the end of the month. I see the 26th was a Saturday. Then it was certainly the 26th.'

Flavières sat down on the arm of an easy chair, close to Gévigne.

'What gave you the idea of coming to me?' he asked.

Again Gévigne wrung his hands. It had been a tic of his in the old days. He had had others—several—but this was the only one left. It was a way of taking hold of himself when he wasn't sure of his foothold.

'I've always thought of you as one of my oldest friends,' he murmured. 'And then I remembered how interested you always were in psychology and all that... You wouldn't have expected me to go to the police, would you?'

Flavières winced, and Gévigne noticed it.

'It was just because you'd left the police that I felt I could come to you about it,' he added.

'Yes,' said Flavières, stroking the leather upholstery, 'I left the police.'

He looked up sharply.

'Do you know why?'

'No. But—'

'You'd find out sooner or later. Things like that can't be kept dark for ever.'

He would have liked to smile, so as to prove his self-possession, but a sour note had already crept into his voice.

'I came a cropper... Another glass of port?'

'No, thanks.'

'It's a rotten story... I was a detective. In the police you have to go right through the mill even if you have a degree. I never liked the job. If my father hadn't pushed me into it... But he was a divisional inspector and for him it was the one and only career. I ought to have refused. It's all wrong to force a boy... but there's no use going into that now... To come to the point, I had to arrest a chap. He wasn't a very dangerous one, only he took it into his head to take refuge on the roof... I had a man called Leriche with me—as nice a fellow as you could meet...'

He emptied his glass. Tears scalded his eyes. He coughed and shrugged his shoulders, trying to recover his poise.

'You see. As soon as this story crops up my feet slip off the pedals,' he said in an attempt to laugh it off. 'The roof was a sloping one. I could hear the traffic a long way below in the street. The chap was behind a chimney. He was unarmed. It was just a matter of collaring him. I couldn't do it.'

'I remember now,' said Gévigne, 'you never had a head for heights.'

'Leriche went in my place. He slipped and fell.'

'Ah!'

Gévigne looked discreetly at the carpet. Flavières studied his face without being able to read his thoughts.

'It's best you should know—'

'Anyone's nerve can give way,' said Gévigne.

'I know it can,' answered Flavières with something like a snarl.

Nothing was said for a moment. Then Gévigne raised his hands in a vague gesture.

'Most unfortunate. But you can't hold yourself responsible because your friend's foot slipped.'

Flavières opened a box of cigarettes.

'Have a fag, old man.'

He always encountered the same bewildered incredulity when he told his story. No one ever took it seriously. How could he ever make them hear Leriche's scream, which went on and on, passing from a shrill note to a lower one with the distance? Perhaps Gévigne's wife too was burdened by some gnawing secret, but it couldn't be half as hideous a one as his. Were her dreams torn by a scream like that? Had she allowed someone to die in her place?

20

Gévigne interrupted this reverie.

'Can I count on you then?'

'What do you want me to do?'

'Have a look at her. Above all I want your opinion. It's already done me a lot of good to talk to you about it. You will help me, won't you?'

'If it is a help.'

'You've no idea how much… Are you free this evening?'

'No.'

'A pity. I'd have asked you home to dinner. It'll have to be another day.'

'No. Better she shouldn't know me. It'll make things easier.'

'Perhaps you're right. But I've got to show her to you somehow.'

'Go to the theatre together. I can have a good look at her without her noticing.'

'Good idea. We're going to the *Marigny* tomorrow. We've got a box.'

'Right. I'll be there.'

Gévigne took both Flavières' hands in his.

'Thanks, Roger… You see how right I was to come to you. You know a trick or two. I shouldn't have thought of the theatre.'

He fumbled in his inside pocket, hesitated.

'Don't be offended… We've still got the dibs to consider… You're doing me a great favour…'

'Oh,' said Flavières, 'never mind about that now.'

'All the same—'

Flavières patted him on the back.

'It's the case I'm interested in, not the money. I've already the feeling your wife and I have something in common, and…

21

yes… there's a chance I may be able to find out what she's hiding.'

'I assure you she's not hiding anything.'

'We'll see.'

Gévigne picked up his grey felt hat and his gloves.

'Business good?'

'Pretty good. I can't complain.'

'You know, if I can be useful to you in any way, you've only to say the word. I'd be only too glad. I'm in touch with some pretty influential people, particularly with this war contract…'

'Profiteer,' thought Flavières.

The word flashed involuntarily into his mind, and he turned away to avoid Gévigne's eye.

'I'm afraid you'll have to use the stairs again. The lift's not working.'

They went out on to the narrow landing. Gévigne leant over to say confidentially to his friend:

'Go about it in your own way. I give you a free hand. As soon as you've anything to tell me, give me a ring at my office, or, better still, come to see me. Our Paris office is in the building next to the *Figaro*… All I ask is that Madeleine is kept absolutely in the dark. She mustn't even suspect anything. If she thought she was being watched… I wouldn't answer for the consequences.'

'Trust me.'

'Thank you.'

Gévigne started down the stairs. Twice he turned to give a friendly wave of the hand. Flavières went back into his office and leant out of the window. He saw a huge black car pull out into the road and glide smoothly away… Madeleine… He liked the name. It had a gentle, plaintive sound. But how could she have brought herself to marry this stocky, corpulent man? Of course she was carrying on with somebody else... Those attacks!... Dragging a red herring across her own tracks... Serve him right. Gévigne deserved to be made a fool of by his wife. Because of his smug affluence, his cigars, his contract for building small craft—because of everything. Flavières didn't like people with too much self-assurance—and, outwardly at least, Gévigne had plenty—though it was a quality he would have given anything to possess himself.

He shut the window irritably. Then he mooched about in the kitchen, trying to persuade himself he was hungry. He surveyed the tins in the cupboard; for he too had laid in a stock of provisions, stupid as he considered such a precaution to be, as by all appearances the war was going to be a short one. Far from tempting him, the sight of so much food made him feel slightly sick. Finally he took some biscuits and the remains of a bottle of wine. He was on the point of sitting down when he decided the kitchen was ugly, and he went, munching, back into the office. As he passed it, he switched on the wireless. He knew beforehand what the *communiqué* would say: Patrol activity, artillery duels here and there on the Rhine. All the same the announcer's voice would be something living.

He sat down. He drank some of the white wine... He hadn't been a success in the police. He wasn't cut out for any service... What was he cut out for?... He opened a drawer and took out a green folder. In the top righthand corner he wrote: *Dossier Gévigne.* Then he slipped a few blank sheets of paper into it, and sat staring in front of him with vacant eyes.

TWO

'It must look pretty silly,' said Flavières to himself.

He certainly felt it as he sat, trying to look distinguished and unconcerned, fidgeting with the mother-of-pearl opera-glasses which he couldn't bring himself to raise to his eyes to study Madeleine's face. There were lots of uniforms round him, and the women with the officers had a look all of their own, proud, satisfied. And Flavières hated them. Now he came to think of it, he hated the army, lock, stock, and barrel, and the war, and this overdecorative theatre which breathed an atmosphere at once martial and frivolous.

He had only to turn his head a little to see Gévigne, who sat with his clasped hands resting on the ledge of the box. Madeleine was sitting back in her chair. She seemed to be dark and slim. Flavières couldn't see her features clearly, but he had the impression she was pretty, with something a bit fragile about her. That might have been due to her abundant hair which seemed too heavy for her face. How could a man like Gévigne have procured a wife of such elegance and grace? How could she have put up with his advances? The curtain went up on a play which Flavières found insipid. He shut his eyes and let his mind run back to the days when he and Gévigne had shared a room to save money. They had been as shy and awkward the one as the other. The women students used to laugh at them, adopting vamping airs just to tease them. They lacked the audacity to cope with girls. Others, on the other hand, seemed able to have any girl they wanted. One in particular. The students called him Marco. He was not remarkably endowed either with brains or good looks. Flavières had once tried to pump him. Marco had smiled, saying:

'Talk to them as though you've already been to bed with them… That's the trick.'

More easily said than done! Flavières lacked the effrontery even to call them *tu* instead of *vous*. And in the police his colleagues used to make fun of him. Nor was it really friendly fun: they didn't take to him—thought him a bit sly. Sometimes they were even a little afraid of him… When had Gévigne finally plucked up his courage? And with what sort of woman? Could it have been with Madeleine? Flavières already called her by her Christian name in his own mind, as though there was already some bond between them, as though they were united in a common hostility to Gévigne.

He tried to picture the dining-room at the *Continental*. He put himself into Gévigne's place, dining with Madeleine for the first time, beckoning the head-waiter, choosing the wines… Ridiculous, of course: he knew very well that one glance from the head-waiter would have made him go hot under the collar… And then… Walking with Madeleine the whole length of the immense dining-room… Upstairs, the bedroom… Madeleine undressing… And finally…

Flavières opened his eyes, fidgeted in his seat. He would have liked to leave the theatre there and then. But he was right in the middle of a row. It would mean disturbing all those people. You needed effrontery for that—the very thing he lacked! There was a ripple of laughter round him; a little burst of applause spread quickly to the whole of the auditorium, then suddenly died out. The actors must have been talking about love. Actors! Flavières shuddered with disgust. Furtively he looked at Madeleine out of the corner of his eye. In that gilded half-light she stood out like a portrait. Jewels glittered on her neck and hung from her ears. Her eyes seemed luminous. She listened with her head slightly to one side, perfectly still, like those unknown beauties admired in the Louvre, the *Mona Lisa, La Belle Ferronière*… Her hair which had a tint of mahogany in it was done in a massive bun on the back of her neck… Mme Gévigne…

Flavières almost lifted his opera-glasses to look at her, but his neighbour was showing obvious signs of irritation. Humbly, Flavières smuggled them back into his pocket and tried to make himself as small as possible. He would leave at the interval. He was certain now of being able to recognize her anywhere. It made him uneasy to think that he was going to follow her, pry into her life. It was of doubtful taste, what Gévigne was asking him to do. Supposing Madeleine found out? After all, she had every right to have a lover if she wanted to. Though he knew he would suffer acutely if he found she had. There was some more applause and a confused murmur of approval. He looked again: Madeleine was sitting in exactly the same position and from the diamonds in her ear-rings came the same steady sparkle. At the corner of her eyes there was a glint of eagerness; her long white hand rested on the red plush ledge, and the box formed a pale gilt frame. All that was lacking was a signature in the corner of the picture. For a second Flavières could almost see one there—the initials R. F. in small red letters. Roger Flavières… No. It was too silly: he wasn't going to fall for that preposterous story of Gévigne's. He mustn't let his imagination run away with him... Perhaps he ought really to have been a novelist, with this host of images which so readily and of their own accord flooded his brain. They weren't vague ones either: they had all the relief, the dramatic intensity of life... That roof, for instance—the shiny wet slates, the discoloured red-brick chimneys, the wisps of smoke all blowing the same way, the rumble of the traffic below, like a torrent at the bottom of a gorge. He wrung his hands, just as Gévigne had done.

If he had chosen the lawyer's profession, it was to discover the secrets that prevent people living. Even Gévigne, with his money, his factories, his influential friends, wasn't really living. They were liars, all of them, these people who, like Marco, pretended they could ride rough-shod over every obstacle. Who knew whether Marco wasn't at that moment in desperate need of a friend to lean on? A man on the stage kissed a girl... It looked so easy, but that was a lie too. Gévigne kissed Madeleine, yet she remained a stranger to him...

The truth was that they were all like him, Flavières, trembling on the edge of a slope at the bottom of which was the abyss. They laughed, they made love, but they were afraid. What would become of them if there weren't whole professions whose job it was to prop them up—the priest's, the doctor's, the lawyer's?

The curtain fell, then rose again. The lights shed a harsh glare which made all the faces look a little grey. People stood up so as to have elbow-room for clapping. Madeleine fanned herself slowly with her programme, while her husband leant over to say something into her ear. Another well-known picture—*La Femme à l'Eventail*. Or was it the portrait of Pauline Lagerlac?

It was certainly better for him to go. He followed the crowd pouring into the corridors and the foyer. For a moment or two he was held up by the crush outside the cloakroom. When he finally got clear, he almost bumped into Gévigne and his wife. He brushed past Madeleine. He had a close-up view of her, yet only realized who she was a moment later. He wanted to look back, but got swept along in a stream of young officers making a dash for the bar. He went down a few steps, still intending to find her again, then suddenly gave it up. He needed to be alone.

He liked those nights of the war, those long deserted avenues, refreshed by a soft, gentle wind which had caressed lawns and smelt of magnolias. He walked noiselessly as a thief. He had no difficulty in recalling Madeleine's face and her dark hair discreetly tinted with henna, and his thoughts lingered over her eyes, intensely blue, but so pale that they didn't seem quite alive, eyes which certainly could never express passion. The cheeks were slightly hollowed out under prominent cheekbones, just sufficiently to harbour a faint shadow which suggested languor. Her mouth was small with hardly any lipstick on it—the mouth of a dreamy child. Madeleine—yes, that was undoubtedly the right name for her. But Gévigne! When she could so well have carried off an aristocratic surname in several pieces, futile but charming. She was unhappy, of course. Gévigne had worked up a ridiculous fable instead of seeing that she was bored to death with him. She was much too delicate, too sensitive, to resign herself to a life of showy luxury. Wasn't it that which had caused her to drop her painting? It was no longer a question of watching her, but of helping her, protecting her.

'There I am, going off the rails again,' he mused. 'If I don't look out I shall find myself in love with her. Madame Gévigne needs a tonic and that's all there is to it!'

He quickened his step, annoyed, vaguely humiliated. By the time he reached home, he had made up his mind to ring Gévigne up and tell him he was called away urgently and would have to chuck up the case. Why should he sacrifice his peace of mind for a man who didn't really care a straw for him? He'd done very well without him for fifteen years, hadn't he? No, he wasn't having any. The Gévignes could go to blazes!

He made himself some camomile tea, saying to himself:

'What would she think of me if she saw me now? A fussy old bachelor encrusted in his solitude and his little fads!'

He had a bad night. On waking, he remembered he was due to follow Madeleine and was mortified by the joy he felt at the prospect. Try as he would, however, he couldn't rid himself of it. It clung to him, humble but obstinate, like a dog you haven't the heart to chase away. He switched on the wireless. More patrol activity! More artillery duels! Good. That wouldn't stop anybody feeling happy. He settled down to his morning's work, whistling.

He lunched at a little restaurant whose customers were all *habitués*. He no longer felt ill at ease to be in civilian clothes—not even when people gave him a dirty look. After all it wasn't his fault that he hadn't got through his medical. He didn't wait till two o'clock to station himself outside the block of flats in the Avenue Kléber. Though the weather had turned fine after a sulky week, there were few people about. Flavières at once spotted the big black car, a Talbot, drawn up in front of the building. He sauntered past it casually.

He took a newspaper out of his pocket and glanced at it idly as he wandered on. Sometimes he actually read a paragraph—a reconnaissance plane shot down in Alsace, reinforcements for

Narvik. What did he care? He was on holiday. He had a tryst with Madeleine! He noticed a little café: three tables on the pavement, a couple of spindle-trees. He sat down.

'A coffee, please.'

He was well placed for studying the building. High windows with complicated mouldings in the style of 1900, a balcony with flowers in pots. Dormer windows in the roof, above which the sky was a watery blue. When his eyes came down to earth again, the Talbot was starting up—Gévigne. Madeleine wouldn't be long now.

He gulped down the scalding coffee, smiling at himself. How did he know she would be coming out this afternoon? Was there any reason why she should?… Yes, there was. She'd come all right. Because of the sunshine, because of the tender green leaves, because of those fluffy seeds floating past on the balmy spring air. Lastly, she'd come because he was waiting for her!

And all of a sudden there she was, standing on the pavement. Flavières promptly dropped his paper, got up and crossed the road. She was wearing a grey suit, very tight at the waist, and her black handbag was tucked under her arm. She looked round her as she finished putting on her gloves. Some delicate white lace fluttered at her throat. Her forehead and eyes were half concealed by a short veil which masked her gracefully. Another portrait! *La Femme au Loup.*

He would have liked to paint that slim silhouette standing in an aura of sunshine, with the pale background of over-ornate architecture. For he too had dabbled in painting in his day. Without much success. The same with the piano. He played just well enough to envy the masters. He was one of those people who hate mediocrity without themselves being able to scale the heights. Plenty of minor talents… plenty of regrets… But never mind about that! Madeleine was there!

She followed the avenue right to the Place du Trocadéro, where she went out on to the terrace of the Palais de Chaillot, whose whiteness was almost blinding. Paris had never looked so like a park. Blue and browny-red, the Eiffel Tower rose up from the lawns, the familiar totem of Parisians. On the near side, the gardens sloped down towards the Seine, surrounding the flights of steps which thus looked like motionless cascades bordered by flowers. A tug blew a raucous blast on its siren, quickly muffled as it swept under a bridge. One seemed here to be suspended between peace and war, gripped by a facile emotion that was nevertheless poignant. Was that why Madeleine was now walking with a certain lassitude? She appeared to hesitate, to be taking herself to task. She stopped in front of the entrance to the museum, then drifted on as though caught by some invisible current. She crossed the Place du Trocadéro, loitered a moment among the people at the end of the Avenue Henri-Martin, then, making up her mind, went into the Cimetière de Passy.

She walked slowly between the gravestones, and Flavières could have sworn she was just continuing her walk. She had branched off almost at once from the central alley with its solemn row of crosses in marble and bronze. She went along the little paths, looking casually about her—at the black lettering on the stones, the rusty railings round a vault, the sudden splash of colour where some flowers had recently been left. Sparrows hopped about in front of her. The roar and clatter of the town seemed to come, filtered, from far away. One might have been transported to some other country on the margin of this life of ours. There was no one to be seen, though many to be felt, each inscription conjuring up an unseen presence.

Amongst them and their stony monuments, Madeleine walked on, her shadow striking between the gravestones or zigzagging up the steps of one of those little chapels over a vault, in which crumbling cherubs kept their vigil. Sometimes she stopped for a moment to read some half-effaced inscription.

FAMILLE MERCIER

ALPHONSE MERCADIER

Il fut bon père et bon époux

There were some gravestones tumbling over sideways like ship-wrecked boats. On others lizards basked in the warmth, their throats palpitating, their serpents' heads lifted towards the sun. Madeleine seemed to feel quite at home in this neglected corner, where no relations ever came. She went on along the path which presently took her right into the heart of the cemetery. She stooped to pick up a red tulip, fallen from a vase, and still with the same leisurely gait went up to one of the graves and stopped. Hidden behind a mausoleum, Flavières was able to watch her at his ease. Madeleine's face showed neither exalta-tion nor sorrow. On the contrary, the expression on it was one of peace and happiness. What thoughts were running through her mind? Her arms hung limply at her sides; her fingers still held the tulip. Once again she looked like a portrait, her whole being turned inwards, lost in some interior contemplation.

The word 'ecstasy' occurred to Flavières. Was this one of those 'attacks' Gévigne had spoken of? Had Madeleine gone off into some sort of mystic trance? No. A mystic trance had certain characteristic symptoms not present here. It was something much simpler: Madeleine must be praying for someone, some member of her family no doubt whose memory was still fresh in her mind, though the tomb looked old enough and quite neglected. That was odd.

Flavières looked at his watch. She had been standing there nearly a quarter of an hour—twelve minutes, to be exact. Now she went back into the central alley, looking around her with the same appearance of being mildly interested, as though in the matter of funereal architecture she had nothing to learn. As he passed, Flavières read the inscription she had been contemplating. It was very short, just:

PAULINE LAGERLAC
1840–1865

That, of course, was the name he had expected, but that didn't make any difference: he was profoundly moved. Gévigne was right: there was something incomprehensible in Madeleine's conduct—in the way she had stood at the grave, for instance, with neither bowed head nor folded hands, much as a person might stand gazing at the house in which he was born.

He brushed aside that absurd idea, which filled him with a vague uneasiness, and hurried on to overtake her. She was still holding the tulip. She walked down towards the Seine. Again she seemed to droop. Perhaps she was just tired. On the quays, she walked as though aimlessly, as though lost in thought, looking at the rippling water sparkling with points of light. It was hot. Men walked by with their hats in their hands, wiping their foreheads. The water was very blue against the grey stone quays, on which a few tramps lay sleeping. The first swallows twittered round the bridges. With her severely cut grey suit and high heels, she looked something of a stranger at the fête, like a traveller waiting for a train. And from time to time she rolled the stalk of the tulip between her fingers.

Crossing the Seine, she stopped on the bridge and leant with her elbows on the parapet, stroking her cheek with the tulip. Had she given someone a rendezvous?… Or was she simply resting?… Perhaps she was only nursing her own ennui, as she watched the swirling wake of a steamer or the fascinating undulations of the reflections in the water… She leant over the parapet, looking at herself far below in the water, with the whole sky above her and the long curve of the bridge cutting across her shoulders.

Flavières came quite close to her, not knowing what impelled him to do so. Madeleine didn't move. She had dropped the tulip, and a little spot of red drifted downstream, turning slowly round and round in the eddies near the bank. It floated past a barge, then farther out into the stream. Flavières found himself, too, getting interested in its fate. The farther it went and the smaller it became, the more impossible was it for him to take his eyes away. Suddenly it was there no longer. Perhaps it had sunk. Madeleine remained, however, staring down at the river. Flavières thought he could see a faint smile on her lips.

She stood up and walked on, returning to the right bank by another bridge. And still with the same unhurried pace and the same indifference to her surroundings, she walked home. It was half past four when she disappeared through the doorway, leaving Flavières high and dry. For that was how he felt—useless, disgusted, not knowing what to do with himself. What on earth was he going to do during the rest of the day? The hours he had spent watching Madeleine made solitude seem unbearable. He went into a café and rang up Gévigne.

'Hallo!… Is that you, Paul?… Roger speaking… Can I drop in on you for a minute or two?… No, nothing's gone wrong. I just wanted to ask you a few more questions… Right. I'll be round in a jiffy.'

Gévigne had spoken casually of his office, like a *grand seigneur*. In reality it took up the whole of one floor of a large building.

'If you wouldn't mind waiting a moment, Monsieur… Monsieur le Directeur is in conference.'

The typist showed him into a comfortably furnished waiting-room. Bluff! thought Flavières. But it wasn't. A moment later he saw Gévigne showing some visitors out.

'Delighted to see you,' said Gévigne when they were alone. 'Sorry to have kept you waiting. We're in a bit of a flap today.'

His room was big and light. It was furnished in American style with filing cabinets and tubular steel armchairs, ash-trays on chromium pedestals. On the wall hung an immense map of Europe with a red cord running in a jagged line round pins, to indicate the present position of the front.

'Well? Have you seen her?'

'Yes.'

'What did she do?'

'She went to a cemetery.'

'Passy?… To the grave of—'

'Yes.'

'You see, Roger!… You see, don't you?'

35

On one corner of the desk, near the telephone, there was a photograph of Madeleine. Flavières couldn't take his eyes off it.

'The gravestone has only one name on it. Aren't her parents...'

'No. They're buried somewhere in the Ardennes. On my side we've a family vault at Saint-Ouen... Pauline Lagerlac is the only relation she's got at Passy. That's what frightens me... Frankly, what do you think of this visit? Can you see any rhyme or reason in it?... And you can be sure it's not the first time she's been there.'

'It certainly didn't look like it. She didn't ask anybody the way. Though she meandered about a bit, she obviously knew where she was going.'

'Of course she did. I tell you she's absolutely obsessed by this Pauline.'

Gévigne paced to and fro behind his desk with his hands in his pockets. On his neck, a roll of fat protruded above his collar. The telephone rang. He snatched up the receiver impatiently. Covering the mouthpiece with his hand, he said quietly:

'She thinks she's Pauline Lagerlac. You can't be surprised if I'm worried about her.'

A muffled voice sounded in the earphone, which he quickly lifted to his ear.

'Hallo!... Yes, Gévigne speaking... Oh, it's you, *cher ami*. I was going to get in touch with you. The thing is—'

Flavières didn't listen. He looked at Madeleine. The face of a statue, the eyes hardly bringing it to life at all. Gévigne barked back his answers, his eyebrows knitted, then banged down the receiver. Flavières was sorry he'd come. He suddenly felt that Madeleine's mystery had to do with herself alone: Gévigne could only obscure the issue. A preposterous idea kept nagging at him: supposing Pauline's soul—

'I lose patience with them,' snarled Gévigne. 'You can't imagine the muddle we're in at the moment. Better you shouldn't! It's discouraging.'

'Is Lagerlac your wife's maiden name?' asked Flavières.

'No. She was called Givors, Madeleine Givors. She lost her mother three years ago. Her father had died not long before. He had paper mills near Mézières. A big concern. Her grandfather founded it. He came from those parts.'

'But Pauline Lagerlac must have lived in Paris, I suppose?'

Gévigne drummed on his blotter with his podgy fingers.

'It's all rather vague, I'm afraid... One day my mother-in-law pointed out an old house in the Rue des Saints-Pères—at least I think it was the Rue des Saints-Pères—saying that it was where her grandmother Pauline had lived. There was a shop on the ground floor—antiques, I believe... But tell me: what do you think of Madeleine now you've seen her?'

Flavières shrugged his shoulders.

'I can't say much yet.'

'But you agree with me that there's something queer about her, don't you?'

'It seems to me... yes... Do you know if she's really given up painting completely?'

'Completely. To the point of doing away with her studio, turning it into an ordinary sitting-room.'

'Why did she drop it?'

'Why indeed?... Of course she's versatile—plenty of interests... And people do change...'

Flavières got up and held out his hand.

'I mustn't take up any more of your time. I can see how busy you are.'

'You mustn't take that line. All this simply doesn't count. Not compared to Madeleine... Honestly, do you think she's mad?'

'Certainly not mad,' answered Flavières. 'Tell me: does she read a lot?'

'No. I wouldn't call her a reader. Like most people, she reads the best-sellers. And magazines.'

'Any special fads or fancies?'

'I can't think of any.'

'I'll keep an eye on her.'

'You don't sound very enthusiastic.'

'I've got such a strong feeling we're wasting our time.'

He didn't want to tell Gévigne he had made up his mind to follow Madeleine week in, week out, for months if necessary; that he wouldn't recover his peace of mind till he'd got to the bottom of the mystery.

'Sorry to put it all on you,' said Gévigne, 'but you see how I'm placed. What with this office and Le Havre, I don't get a minute to myself. It took a load off my mind when you took on the job.'

He led Flavières out to the lift.

'Give me a ring if you find out anything.'

'All right. I will.'

In the street Flavières found himself in the six o'clock rush. He bought an evening paper. Two enemy planes had been brought down near the Luxemburg frontier. The leading article proved conclusively that the Germans were losing the war. They were blockaded; they were contained. The General

Staff had envisaged every possibility and were only waiting for the enemy to embark on a last despairing venture.

Flavières yawned and stuffed the paper into his pocket. He couldn't take any further interest in this war. What mattered was Madeleine. He took a seat on the terrace of a café and ordered some mineral water… Madeleine dreaming in front of Pauline's tomb… Homesick! For the grave!… No, it was impossible. But who really knew what was possible or not?

He went home with a headache. He turned over the pages of his encyclopaedia—the volume with the L's, of course— and naturally found nothing. He knew very well the name of Lagerlac wouldn't be mentioned, but he couldn't have gone to sleep before making sure. An off-chance, but it had to be checked… He had a feeling he was going to do lots of silly things 'on the off-chance', from now on. He had only to think of her to lose his sense of proportion. *La femme à la tulipe!* He tried to make a sketch of her, leaning over the parapet, staring at the river. No good. He crumpled up the sheet of paper and took a couple of aspirins.

THREE

Madeleine walked past the Chambre des Députés, in front of which a sentry, with fixed bayonet, was pacing up and down. As on the previous afternoon, she had left the house almost immediately after Gévigne. This time, however, she walked quickly, and Flavières kept close on her heels, afraid she would be run over, for she sailed across the road without the least regard for the traffic. Where was she going to in such a hurry? She was dressed quite differently today. Instead of her smart grey suit, she wore a very ordinary brown one, with a simple beret on her head. But that only made her look younger: there was something of the bachelor girl about her. She took the Boulevard Saint-Germain, keeping to the shady side. Was she making for the Luxembourg? Or the Salle de Géographie? To a lecture on occultism, perhaps, or a *séance*.

All at once Flavières understood. He drew closer behind her, to be all the more sure of not losing her.

He could smell her perfume. A complicated smell, which had affinities with rich earth and dead flowers. Where had he come across it before? The previous day, of course, in the deserted part of the Cimetière de Passy… He liked it. It reminded him of his grandparents' house near Saumur, built on the side of a steep rocky hill with caves in it. People lived in the caves. To reach their houses, they had, like Robinson Crusoe, to use a ladder. Here and there a stovepipe peeped out of the rock, and above it a long smudge of black stained the white stone. During his holidays he had loved to explore this strange settlement, peering in through the openings at the beautifully polished furniture inside. Once he had gone into one of those dwellings that had been abandoned. Only a little light penetrated to the far end of the cave. The walls were cold and gritty and the silence was terrifying. At night they must have been able to hear moles burrowing in the ground, and perhaps an occasional worm would fall writhing from the ceiling. A rickety door at the back led into the 'basement' which was rank with mouldy air. He hadn't dared explore further into the forbidden world of galleries and passages which ramified in all directions, extending beyond the sprawling clumps of grey toadstools growing just beyond that door.

The whole place was imbued with that scent—the scent of Madeleine. And there on the sunny boulevard under the budding trees, Flavières experienced once again the fearful attraction of the shades, and he understood why, at the first glance, Madeleine had touched him.

Another image surged into his brain. At the age of twelve, under the shadow of that hill, he had read a translation of that unforgettable book of Kipling's *The Light that Failed*. The frontispiece was a picture of a boy and a girl who were leaning over a revolver, and the absurd caption had remained in his mind and had never failed to bring tears to his eyes: *C'était the Barralong qui faisait route vers l'Afrique Australe…* The young girl, dressed in black, resembled Madeleine—he was sure of it now—and had made no less an impression on him. He had thought about her as he went to sleep and heard her footsteps in his dreams.

All this was ridiculous, of course. It would be, at any rate to a man like Gévigne. On another level it was true enough, with the truth of a lost dream found once again and full of mysterious evidence. Madeleine walked in front of him, a slim dark figure, a prey to the shadows, smelling of chrysanthemums. When she turned down the Rue des Saints-Pères, Flavières felt a sort of bitter satisfaction. Of course that didn't prove anything, either. And yet…

There was the house Gévigne had spoken of. It must be that one, because there was an antique shop on the ground floor, and because Madeleine at once went in through the entrance at the side of it. There was only one thing which didn't tally with Gévigne's description: the house from the first floor upwards was a hotel. An English name: *Family Hotel*. It couldn't have more than twenty rooms by the look of it. A card hung at the door bearing the word *complet*. Flavières went in. An old woman knitting at the reception desk looked at him over her glasses.

'No, I don't want a room,' said Flavières. 'I merely wanted to know the name of the woman who has just come in.'

'Who are you?'

Flavières held out his old card giving his status as a detective. He had kept it as he kept everything: old pipes, broken fountain pens, and documents that were no longer of the slightest interest. His wallet was stuffed with yellowing letters, receipts for registered packets, old coupons and counterfoils. For once he could congratulate himself on this otherwise foolish habit. The old woman, still looking askance at him, answered:

'Madeleine Gévigne.'

'This isn't the first time you've seen her, is it?'

'Oh no. She often comes.'

'Does she have a… a visitor in her room?'

'She's a most respectable lady.'

Looking down at her knitting, she smiled knowingly.

'Would you mind answering my question? Does she see people here, friends or otherwise?'

'No. No one has ever come to see her here.'

'Then what does she do here?'

'I don't know. I don't spy on my customers.'

'What's the number of her room?'

'Nineteen. It's on the third floor.'

'Is it one of your best rooms?'

'No, though it's comfortably furnished. I offered her No. 12, but she wouldn't look at it. She wanted the room on the third floor which gave on to the yard. It was that or nothing.'

'Why?'

'She didn't say. It's a sunny room—perhaps it was that.'

'She keeps the room permanently, does she?'

'She has it by the month. At least, she took it for one month.'

'When did she come?'

The old woman stopped knitting and turned over the pages of the register.

'Three weeks ago, I think. Yes, here we are—April 5th.'

'Does she stay long in her room as a rule?'

'Sometimes an hour, sometimes two.'

'Has she got any things up there?'

'No. She's never brought any luggage.'

'She doesn't come every day, does she?'

'No. Two or three times a week.'

'Have you ever thought there was anything queer about her?'

The old woman pushed her glasses up on to her forehead and rubbed her wrinkled eyes.

'Everybody's queer in one way or another,' she said. 'If you'd spent your life at the reception desk of a hotel, you wouldn't ask such a question.'

'Does she use the telephone?'

'No.'

'How long has this house been a hotel?'

'For the last fifty years.'

'What was it before?'

'A private house, I suppose, like the others.'

'Have you ever heard of a certain Pauline Lagerlac?'

'No. Do you want me to search the register?'

'That would be useless.'

For a moment they looked at each other in silence.

'Thank you,' said Flavières.

'Don't mention it!' said the other a little tartly, and went back to her knitting.

Flavières didn't go at once. For another minute he stood with his elbow on the desk, fidgeting with the lighter in his pocket.

'I've lost the knack,' he thought. 'I no longer know how to squeeze the truth out of people.'

He would have liked to go up and look through the keyhole of No. 19, but he knew very well he would see nothing. With a nod and a grunt to the old woman, he turned and went out.

Why had it got to be the back room on the third floor? Unless in its day it had been Pauline Lagerlac's bedroom. Only, if it had been, Madeleine couldn't possibly know it. She didn't even know of the woman's suicide... In that case?... What mysterious appeal could have brought her to this particular

44

room in this particular house? Various explanations occurred to him—clairvoyance for instance—but he rejected them one after the other. Madeleine was a perfectly normal woman: there were specialists to vouch for it... No. The answer had to be sought for in some other quarter.

At the corner of the Boulevard Saint-Germain he looked back, and he almost broke into a run at the sight of Madeleine walking in the opposite direction, down towards the Seine. She had been in the hotel barely half an hour. Walking briskly along the quays, she passed the Gare d'Orsay, then suddenly hailed a taxi. Flavières just had time to secure another.

'Follow that Renault,' he shouted, jumping in.

Perhaps he ought to have brought his own car. Madeleine had almost given him the slip.

On the Pont de la Concorde and all up the Champs-Elysées the traffic was as thick as on the busiest days before the war. Madeleine's taxi was heading towards the Etoile. She was obviously going home. There were uniforms everywhere and big cars flying pennants as on Bastille Day. There was something a little feverish about it all which even Flavières couldn't ignore. He didn't really dislike this sensation of slightly heightened life on the brink of danger... No. She wasn't going home. The taxi rounded the Arc de Triomphe and then went straight on down the Avenue de Neuilly towards the Porte Maillot. The cars were less numerous here; they dawdled along with windows down and roofs open.

'Seems they're going to cut down the petrol ration, even for taxis,' observed the driver.

Flavières said to himself that, thanks to Gévigne, he'd get all the coupons he wanted. He reproached himself for the thought, then proceeded to smother his conscience—a gallon or two more or less in the wholesale wastage would make no difference to anyone.

'Drop me here, will you?'

Madeleine was getting out at the far end of the Pont de Neuilly. Flavières had his money all ready in his hand, so as not to lose a moment, but this time Madeleine sauntered off with as leisurely a pace as on the previous day. She walked along the quays, apparently with no aim in view, just for the pleasure of walking. It was impossible to think of any link between the hotel in the Rue des Saints-Pères and the Quai de Courbevoie. If she just wanted to walk, why come all this way? The quays in the centre of Paris were far more beautiful. Was it the need to get away from the crowd? If she wanted to think something out, or merely to dream, it was certainly quiet enough here beside the smoothly flowing river. He thought of the days when he had wandered along the banks of the Loire, with its little islands, its tongues of sand, hot underfoot, the osier-beds in which the frogs croaked out their joy at being alive. Madeleine was like him: he felt sure of it; and he was tempted to overtake her. They wouldn't need to talk. They would simply walk side by side watching the barges gliding through the water. It wouldn't do, of course, and to curb the impulse he stopped altogether and allowed her to get well ahead. He even thought of going home. But there was something a little intoxicating and more than a little questionable in this pursuit which fascinated him, obsessed him. He went on.

Heaps of sand, heaps of stones, then more heaps of sand… Here and there a rustic wharf, a crane, some tip-trucks on narrow rusty rails. They were opposite the Ile de la Grande Jatte.

What was she doing in this dismal suburb? Where was she leading him? They were all alone there, one behind the other, yet she showed no sign whatever of being conscious of his existence. She was too absorbed in the river to look behind her.

Little by little, Flavières was assailed by a vague fear. No, she wasn't out for a walk. Was this some eccentric escapade? Or an attack of amnesia? He knew something of the latter, as the police often had to deal with people who had lost their memories, strange bewildered people who spoke like sleep-walkers. He was overtaking her again. They were approaching an isolated building, one of those little *bistrots* which cater for bargees. Outside it were three iron tables under a discoloured sunblind. She sat down at one of them. Flavières hid behind a stack of barrels on the quay, but without taking his eyes off her.

She took a piece of paper out of her bag, and a fountain pen. With the back of her hand she made sure the table wasn't wet. The innkeeper didn't put in an appearance. She wrote carefully, her features slightly puckered.

'She loves someone,' thought Flavières, 'someone who's been called up.'

But that supposition was worth no more than the others. Nor did it explain why she should come all this way to write a letter she could have written just as easily—more clandes-tinely, in fact—at home. Her pen went steadily on; she never paused to grope for a word. Perhaps she had been composing the letter in her head while walking. Or during that half-hour at the hotel. Suppositions again! Really he had nothing to go on… Was she breaking with Gévigne?… That might explain her restless ambulations. Not her visit to Pauline Lagerlac's grave, however.

No one came to serve her. The innkeeper was no doubt at the front, like the others. Madeleine folded up her letter, put it in an envelope, addressed it, and carefully licked it up. She looked round her, rapped on the table to attract attention. Still no one came. Finally she got up, holding her letter in her hand. Was she going to retrace her steps? She hesitated. Flavières would have given anything to have been able to read the name on the envelope.

Still uncertain, she wandered down to the edge of the quay, passing quite close to the barrels, so close that once again he caught a whiff of her perfume. A soft breeze was blowing, just strong enough to make her skirt flutter. Her face, side-view, was calm. If there was any expression on it at all, it was one of discouragement. She looked down, turned the envelope over, then suddenly tore it in two, in four, and finally into tiny pieces, which she scattered in the breeze. They fluttered down, some on to the stone coping, some on to the water, where they floated for a while; and she stood gravely contemplating them. She rubbed her thumb against her forefinger as though wanting to rid herself of an undesirable contact. With the toe of her shoe, she extricated some fragments caught up in a tuft of grass, and they too disappeared. Quite calmly she took a step forward.

The splash came up right on to the quay, almost wetting Flavières' feet.

'Madeleine!'

For a moment, Flavières stood where he was, non-plussed. The last fragments of the letter had blown into the water except one solitary bit which fluttered along the quay, stopping, then going on again in sudden spurts, like a white mouse.

Madeleine!

He threw off his jacket and waistcoat and rushed towards the edge. A ring of wavelets was still spreading out across the river. He dived in. The cold took his breath away. But that didn't stop her name welling up to his lips from the very centre of his being.

Madeleine! Madeleine!

For a second or two he floundered in the dirty water, then came to the surface. Madeleine had already drifted a few yards downstream. She was on her back, floating, looking already like a drowned person. By the time he reached her—puffing and spluttering, his eyes stinging, his limbs heavy—she seemed to be nothing but a dark shapeless object, slowly sinking. He grabbed her clothes, fumbled for her neck. Yes, that was the thing—he must at all costs keep her head up.

He found her head, and with one arm around it began swimming towards the bank. They made slow progress. How heavy she was! Had she already become rooted in this river? The quay swept rapidly past as they were carried down on the stream. It wasn't far, but he felt his strength ebbing away and he was panting for breath. He had never bothered to keep himself physically fit. He took the air in great gasps, sometimes with half a mouthful of water.

He saw some steps, with a boat moored up alongside. He must at all costs reach those steps before they were swept past. It was a near thing. He just managed to grab the mooring chain of the boat and haul himself along till his feet found the steps submerged beneath the water.

It was a job hauling Madeleine out. He laboured up, one step at a time. A cascade of water gushed out of their clothes. When she was just clear of the water, he let her lie on the steps for a minute. When she had drained off a bit she would be lighter, he thought. Besides, he had to consider how to carry her up. Finally he bent down and just managed to lift her, and, half carrying her, half dragging her, he got her to the top. There, he collapsed himself, exhausted. It was Madeleine who moved first. Realizing she had stirred, he collected himself, sat up, and looked at her. She was a pitiful sight, her hair plastered on her cheeks, her skin blotchy. Her eyes were open, gazing pensively at the sky, as though trying to recognize something.

'You're not dead,' said Flavières simply.

The eyes turned towards him, her thoughts seemed to come back from some other world.

'I don't know,' she said softly. 'It doesn't hurt to die.'

'Fool!' cried Flavières. 'Come on. Pull yourself together.'

He put his hands under her arms and lifted her. Her body was quite limp, so he threw her over his shoulder. He didn't find her heavy now, and the little café wasn't far. All the same, his knees were wobbling when he reached it. He took her inside.

'Hallo! Is anyone there?'

He put Madeleine down on her feet in front of the bar. She was able to stand, if unsteadily. Her teeth chattered.

'Hey, there!'

'Coming. Coming,' answered a voice and a woman emerged from behind the scenes, carrying a baby.

'There's been an accident,' explained Flavières. 'Do you think you could lend us some clothes? It doesn't matter what. You see the state we're in.'

He laughed awkwardly, trying to reassure the woman. The baby began to howl.

'He's teething,' she said, rocking him gently.

'If we could just get into dry clothes, I'll get a taxi to take us home... I've left my wallet in my jacket on the quayside. I'll go and fetch it... Meanwhile, will you make Madame a hot grog... and make it strong?'

He was trying to pass it off as easily as possible, both to allay any misgivings on the woman's part and to help Madeleine get back to her normal self. On his side, he was now overflowing with joy, energy, and decisiveness.

'Sit down,' he said peremptorily to Madeleine.

He quickly crossed the deserted quay to the stack of barrels and recovered his jacket and waistcoat. A ducking at that time of the year wasn't a very serious matter, but, with the river running strongly, it had been a near thing... What chiefly stuck in his mind, however, was not the effort he had had to make nor the dread he had felt, but the vision of Madeleine calmly stepping over the brink. And then, in the water, she hadn't struggled: she had immediately abandoned herself to the river, with a resignation that was something monstrous. If death had come to her, she simply wouldn't have noticed it! He swore a mental oath never to let her out of his sight. From now on he would protect her against herself. She needed protection. She wasn't quite normal, he felt sure of that now. He went back to the *bistrot* at the run, trying to get warm. The woman, with the baby still on her arm, was filling two glasses.

'Where is she?'

'In the next room, changing.'

'Can I use the telephone?'

'Yes. It's over there.'

She jerked her chin towards the far end of the bar. He rang up for a taxi.

'I've got some blue trousers and a jersey,' she said when he rang off. 'Will that do?'

'Perfectly.'

At that moment, Madeleine came out of the kitchen, and he got another shock. In a cheap print dress, her bare feet in sandals, she was another Madeleine altogether, and one that was not in the least intimidating.

'Go and change at once,' she said. '… Really, I'm awfully sorry… Another time I'll be more careful.'

'I sincerely hope there won't be another time,' grumbled Flavières.

He had expected her to thank him. It was to have been a rather touching scene. And here she was being jocular about it! Furious, he muttered to himself as he changed into clothes that were several sizes too big for him. He was going to look ridiculous into the bargain. In the bar the two women were hobnobbing together in an undertone. As thick as thieves! His joy had completely evaporated, and when he found the blue trousers to be covered with streaks of black grease he was angrier than ever. Against Gévigne. He'd pay for this! And he could have his wife watched by someone else in future. A motor-horn sounded outside. That was the taxi. Red and discomfited, he went back into the bar.

'Are you ready?'

Madeleine was holding the baby.

'Hush!' she said. 'You'll wake him.'

She handed the baby very gently back to his mother and this solicitude still further exasperated Flavières. Hardly able to contain himself, he gathered up his wet clothes, put some money on the table, and stumped out. Madeleine ran after him.

'Where can I drop you?' he asked coldly.

She got into the taxi.

'We'd better go to your place first,' she said. 'I expect you're in a hurry to get back into decent clothes. It doesn't matter about me.'

'Tell me where you live, all the same.'

'Avenue Kléber... I'm Madame Gévigne... My husband's a ship-builder.'

'I'm a lawyer. Maître Flavières.'

He opened the sliding glass panel between him and the driver.

'Rue de Maubeuge. Drop us at the corner of the Rue Lamartine.'

'I'm afraid you're angry with me,' said Madeleine. 'I really don't know what happened.'

'I do. You tried to kill yourself.'

He paused, expecting her to make excuses. As she didn't answer, he went on:

'You can have confidence in me. I'm quite ready to understand. You've been dragging some sorrow about with you... a disappointment perhaps?...'

'No,' she said softly. 'It's not what you think.'

Once again she was the person he'd seen at the theatre, *La Femme à l'Eventail*; once again she was the person who had stood lost in meditation at that neglected grave.

'I wanted to throw myself into the water,' she said, 'but I swear I don't know why.'

'Come on! What about that letter?'

She reddened.

'It was for my husband. But what I was trying to explain to him was so extraordinary that in the end—'

She turned towards Flavières and laid a hand on his arm.

'Do you think it's possible to live again, Monsieur?... I mean... is it possible to die and then... live again in someone else?... You see! You don't want to answer. You think I'm mad.'

'Look here.'

'I'm not mad, I assure you... But I can't shake off the feeling that my past goes back a long way—much further than my memories of childhood. Beyond the little girl I remember, there's another life, as it were, a life I'm only beginning to recollect... But I don't know why I'm telling you all this.'

'Go on,' urged Flavières. 'Go on.'

'I can recall things I've certainly never seen. Not with my own eyes. Often faces; sometimes scenes. And occasionally I have quite definitely the impression I'm an old, old woman.'

She had a deep contralto voice. Flavières sat quite rigid, listening to her.

'I suppose it's some kind of an illness,' she sighed. 'Yet, if it was, I can't believe those recollections would be so vivid. They'd be vague and incoherent.'

'But this afternoon did you give way to a sudden impulse or had you thought it out beforehand?'

'I suppose it was a deliberate intention. That's not very clear however... I have increasingly the feeling that I'm a stranger here, that my real life lies behind me. If it does, what's the point of going on with this one?... For you—and for everyone else, in fact—life's the exact opposite of death... For me...'

'You shouldn't talk like that. Think of your husband.'

'Poor Paul! If he knew!'

'He mustn't. This must remain a secret between us two.'

Flavières couldn't help putting a note of tenderness into the words, and she smiled at him, suddenly, with a disconcerting vivacity.

'You're right,' she said. 'It must be a professional secret. Thanks for reassuring me... It was a stroke of luck for me that you happened to be there on the quay.'

'It was indeed. I was going to see a client whose works are a little farther on. If it hadn't been such a lovely day, I should certainly have taken my car.'

'And I'd have been dead by now.'

The taxi stopped.

'Here we are,' said Flavières. 'You'd better come in. I'm afraid the place is in a bit of a mess. I'm a bachelor, and much too busy to look after myself properly.'

They didn't meet anybody either in the hall or on the stairs. Flavières was thankful for that. He didn't want anybody to see him in those clothes. The telephone was ringing as he opened his door and ushered Madeleine in.

'One of my clients, I expect. Sit down. Excuse me a moment.'

He hurried into his office ahead of her.

'Hallo!'

It was Gévigne.

'I've already tried twice to get through to you. I suddenly thought of something I didn't tell you... About Pauline Lagerlac's suicide. She drowned herself. I don't know whether it's any use, but I thought you ought to know... And on your side? Any news?'

'I'll tell you when we meet,' answered Flavières. 'I must ring off now. I've got a client with me.'

FOUR

Flavières looked sulkily at his memorandum book. May 6th. Three appointments—two probates and a divorce. He'd had about enough of this stupid way of earning a living. A shop-keeper could simply put up his shutters and take a day off. Any number of days. For politeness' sake, he stuck up a little notice: *Fermé pour cause de mobilisation,* or any other reason he liked to invent, and no one cared two hoots. But clients were different to customers. They had rights—the right to ring you up at any hour of the day. And they would. He'd have to listen attentively, making notes. And the one at Orléans would once again press Flavières to go and see him. Then in the late afternoon, Gévigne would ring up or call round to see him. He was exacting. You couldn't get rid of the man till you'd told him every single detail.

Sitting at his desk, Flavières opened the *Dossier Gévigne* and went idly through the diary of the last few days. *April 27th. Walk in the Bois de Boulogne. 28th. Paramount Cinema. 29th. Outing. Rambouillet and the Chevreuse valley. 30th. Marignan. Tea on the terrace on top of the Galeries Lafayette. Felt a bit giddy so high up, and we had to come down. She laughed a lot. May 1st. Trip to Versailles. She drives well, and the Simca's inclined to be capricious. 2nd. Forêt de Fontainebleau. 3rd. Didn't see her. 4th. Stroll in the Jardin du Luxembourg. 5th. Long drive in the country. Glimpse of Chartres Cathedral…*

And today, on May 6th, he was later to write: *I'm in love with her. I couldn't live without her.* For that's how things would stand from now on. A melancholy love like a fire smouldering in an abandoned mine. Madeleine appeared to suspect nothing. She regarded him as a friend, that was all, a pleasant companion with whom she could talk freely. No question, of course, of introducing him to Paul! Flavières did his best to play the part of a man of private means who dabbled in law to give himself something to do, and who was delighted with the job of helping a pretty woman to pass the time away.

The accident—if you could call it an accident—at Courbevoie was forgotten. At least it was never referred to. It had not been without its effects—it had given him a certain authority over her—and she knew how to greet him in a way which said as plainly as words that he had saved her life. She was attentive and considerate, as she might have been to any uncle or guardian. A word of love would have been indelicate! Besides, there was Gévigne. And Flavières made it a point of honour to report to him every evening, telling him exactly what they had done. Gévigne would listen to the end, frowning; then they would once again discuss Madeleine's strange affliction.

Flavières shut the folder, stretched his legs out and folded his hands on the desk… Madeleine's affliction… Twenty times a day he turned it over in his mind, examining every action, every attitude, every word she had spoken. She wasn't ill. Yet there was something wrong with her. On the one hand she seemed thoroughly to enjoy life: she loved the whirl and bustle of the crowd; she was gay, sometimes exuberant; her conversation was lively and amusing, and anyone would have at once put her down as a happy person. That was the bright side of the picture. The other was nocturnal, murky, mysterious. On this side she was cold, remaining quite untouched by what went on around her and quite incapable of any real volition, let alone passion.

Gévigne was quite right: as soon as you stopped entertaining her, holding her back into this life, she sank into a sort of numbness which was neither meditation nor gloom, but a subtle change of state. It was as though her soul might at any minute float away and gradually dissipate itself in the wind. Several times Flavières had seen her slip silently into this condition as she sat with him, like a medium whose real self has been summoned to another world.

'Anything the matter?' he would say.

A flicker, as of recognition, would pass over her face, and, with a vague, hesitant smile and a tentative groping, as it were, for her own muscular powers and reflexes, she would slowly come to the surface. There she would blink for a second, then say:

'No. I'm quite all right.'

And the look in her eyes would reassure him.

One day, perhaps, she would open up and tell him more about herself. Meanwhile he was cautious. He rarely let her drive, for instance. She did it very well, but with a sort of fatalism. She lacked the instinct of self-preservation, ready to take whatever came. He was reminded of a time when he had been under treatment for blood-pressure. The slightest movement had cost him an effort. If he had seen a thousand-franc note on the floor, he couldn't have bothered to pick it up. It was like that with Madeleine—as though a spring had broken. And, if in fact she drove well, he could never rid himself of the feeling that, suddenly faced by an obstacle, she wouldn't trouble to avoid it, would simply *accept* it... At Courbevoie, she hadn't struggled in the water.

Another thing: when they went for a drive, she never chose their destination. If he offered her a choice, she would dodge it, saying she didn't mind, that it was all the same to her. Yet this apparent indifference would be, the next moment, belied by her obvious enjoyment. Laughing, her cheeks flushed, she would squeeze his arm, and he would be conscious of her body full of vitality. Sometimes he couldn't help murmuring:

'You're wonderful.'

'Really?'

At such moments, when she looked at him with those pale blue eyes which seemed to have been slightly blinded by the light of day, he would feel an almost painful constriction round the heart.

She tired quickly, and was always hungry. At four o'clock she was already on the look-out for a place where they could have tea. Flavières didn't like to take her to the *pâtisseries* or the *salons de thé*. That's why he took her as often as possible out into the country. To sit in one of those places in wartime eating a *baba* or a *millefeuille* made him feel acutely self-conscious. He was convinced the waitresses, each with a husband or a lover at the front, were looking at him contemptuously. On the other hand he understood only too well why Madeleine should need more food than other people to keep her alive. Once, when they were having tea together, he said:

'You remind me of Aeneas.'

'Why?'

'Don't you remember? When he went down to the nether world, he poured blood on the ground all round him. And the shades came and sniffed at it and the smell of it gave them for a moment a semblance of consistency, and they chattered and chattered…'

'But what's that got to do with me?'

He pushed over to her the plateful of *croissants*.

'Go on—eat them up, all of them. I can't help feeling that you too lack substance. So go on eating, little Eurydice!'

She smiled with a crumb sticking to the corner of her mouth.

'You'll be getting me worried with all your mythology!'

And, after a long pause, putting her cup down, she asked:

'All the same, it's a nice name… Eurydice!… And you did bring me back from the nether world, didn't you?'

But instead of to the Seine and the muddy quay, his mind went back to those cave-dwellings near the Loire, whose deathly silence was only broken by the monotonous drip of water. He put his hand on hers.

From that day he playfully called her Eurydice. He would never have dared call her Madeleine. Besides, Madeleine was a married woman, another man's wife. Eurydice belonged to him and him alone. He had held her in his arms! In the water, admittedly, and with the shadow of death on her face…

He was making a fool of himself, of course. Torturing himself into the bargain, living in a constant tumult of painful impressions. Never mind! Beneath that tumult was a peace and a plenitude of joy such as he had never known. It swallowed up the frustrations of recent years, the fears, the regrets. What a long time he had waited for this woman who was not quite at home in the daylight! Since the age of twelve, to be exact, when he had first penetrated into the heart of the earth, exploring the shadows, the country of phantoms, of the dead…

The telephone rang. He snatched up the receiver eagerly, knowing who it was, and said:

'Hallo, it's you, is it?… Free?… Yes, I think I could make it… Oh yes, I've plenty to do, but none of it's very urgent… Sure you want to?… Fine; but I ought to be back by five… Where shall we go?… About time you chose something… All right. What about a museum or a gallery?… Not very original I admit. A sentimental stroll through the Louvre?… No, they haven't taken everything away. There are quite a lot of good things left. All the more reason to go while we still have the chance… Right. Thanks. At two o'clock, then.'

He put the receiver down very gently, as though a last echo of her voice was still lingering in it. What would the day bring forth? Nothing in all probability. Nothing, that is to say, which took him any nearer to a solution of the problem. There wasn't one: they were in a blind alley. Madeleine would never be cured: there was no use pretending she would. Her mind might be less bent on suicide now that he was going about with her, but that didn't make her at bottom any different. An obsessional type. What ought he to say to Gévigne? Ought he to tell him bluntly she was a hopeless case?…

Flavières had been over every inch of this ground, and once again his thoughts were going round in the same inevitable circle. It was paralysing. He felt incapable of getting his mind out of the rut, incapable of the least mental effort.

Picking up his hat, he went out. His clients would come back another day—or not at all! It didn't matter in the slightest. What did? Paris might at any moment be reduced to a heap of rubble. Besides, if the war went on, he would probably feel obliged to join up in some capacity or other. The future was in any case a blank. Nothing had any real meaning except the present, the spring leaves in the sunshine—and love. Instinctively he made for the Grands Boulevards, needing the noise and the bustle, to rub shoulders with the throng. There perhaps he could for a moment forget Madeleine. He needed that more than anything! Sauntering about near the Opéra, he realized the extent to which he was in her clutches. She absorbed literally all his strength. He was a blood-donor. No, that wasn't the word. A soul-donor.

It left him so empty that, left alone, he had to jostle with the crowd to replenish his nervous system. At first he thought of nothing with any continuity, just letting ideas flit idly through his brain… Whatever the war did to him, he somehow felt sure he would survive… Then he began to dream: Gévigne died, leaving Madeleine free. That of course was a pleasant daydream, and he basked in imaginary situations, worked out to the last detail… Soon he was enjoying a marvellous freedom from earthly cares, like an opium-smoker. The crowd rocked him gently in its lap. He surrendered himself, taking a day off from the exacting business of being a man.

He stopped to look into Lancel's window. Not that he wanted to buy anything. He loved to contemplate jewels and shining gold against a background of dark velvet. Suddenly he remembered that Madeleine had broken her lighter. There were several on a glass shelf, cigarette-cases too, made of all sorts of precious materials. She couldn't be offended. He went in and bought a tiny lighter of very pale gold and a cigarette-case of Russian leather. For once, he actually enjoyed spending money. Asking for a card, he wrote on it: *A Eurydice ressuscitée*, and slipped it in the cigarette-case. He would give her the little parcel at the Louvre, or perhaps later when they had a light dinner together before separating. The morning was embellished by this purchase. He smiled every time he was conscious of the packet tied up with a blue ribbon. Dear, dear Madeleine!

At two he was waiting at the Etoile. She was always punctual.

'Ah!' he exclaimed. 'You're in black today.'

'I love black. If I had my own way I'd wear nothing else.'

'Why? It's a bit mournful, isn't it?'

'Not at all. On the contrary, it gives value to everything; it makes all one's thoughts more important and obliges one to take oneself seriously.'

'And if you were in blue, or green?'

'I don't know. I might think myself a river or a poplar… When I was little, I thought colours had mystical properties. Perhaps that's what made me want to paint.'

She took his arm, with an abandon that almost submerged him in a wave of tenderness.

'I've tried my hand at painting too,' he said. 'The trouble is, my drawing's always so weak.'

'What does that matter? It's the colour that counts.'

'I'd love to see your paintings.'

'They're not worth much. You couldn't make head or tail of them: they're dreams really… Do you dream in colour?'

'No. Everything's grey. Like a photograph.'

'Then you couldn't understand. You're one of the blind!'

She laughed and squeezed his arm to show him she was only teasing.

'Dreams are so much more beautiful than the stuff they call reality,' she went on. 'Imagine a profusion of interweaving colours which penetrate right into you, filling you so completely that you become like one of those insects which make themselves indistinguishable from the leaf they're resting on… Every night I dream of… of the other country.'

'You too!'

Pressed close together, they skirted the Place de la Concorde, not looking at anybody. Flavières hardly knew in what direction his feet were taking him. He was lost in the sweetness of this intimacy, though another part of him was alert and watchful, never losing sight of the problem.

'When I was a boy I was obsessed myself by that unknown world. If we had a map here I could show you the exact spot where it begins.'

'That's not the same one.'

'Oh yes, it is. My end of it is dark, yours full of colour, but they join. It's the same world.'

'That's when you were a boy. You don't believe in it any longer, do you?'

Flavières hesitated. But she looked at him so trustfully, and she seemed to attach so much importance to his answer, that he couldn't help saying:

'Yes, I do… Particularly since I've known you.'

They walked on for a little way in silence—walking in step seemed to make them think in concert. They crossed the immense forecourt of the Louvre and went up some narrow steps and through a dark entrance. Soon they were sauntering among Egyptian gods in the coolness of a cathedral.

'With me, it's not a question of belief,' she began again. 'I know… That world is just as real as this one. Only, one mustn't say so.'

The statues, their feet one behind the other, looked at them with their great blank eyes. Here and there were sarcophagi gleaming like cellophane, blocks of stone covered with indecipherable inscriptions, and, in the solemn depth of the vast rooms, grimacing faces, heads of animals scratched and worn down by the ages, a whole fauna of monstrous, petrified forms.

'I've already walked through these rooms on the arm of a man,' she murmured. 'That was long ago, very long ago... He was like you, only he had sidewhiskers.'

'That's an illusion, no doubt. It's a well-known one, the "seen-it-before" illusion, and quite common.'

'I don't think it is. I could give you details with startling precision. For instance, I often see a little town whose name I couldn't give you—I don't even know whether it is in France—and in my reveries I walk through it as if I had always lived there... A river runs through the middle of it... On the right bank there's a Gallo-Roman triumphal arch, and if you go up an avenue of huge plane-trees you see an amphitheatre on your left, some vaults and crumbling steps. Behind the amphitheatre, I can see three poplar trees and a herd of sheep...'

'But... but I know that town,' cried Flavières. 'It's Saintes and the river's the Charente.'

'Maybe.'

'But they've cleared the ground round the amphitheatre. You wouldn't see any poplars now.'

'There used to be some... in my time... And the little fountain—is that still there?... Girls used to throw pins into the water wishing they'd be married within the year.'

'The fountain of St. Estelle!'

'And the church, behind the amphitheatre... a tall church, with a very old tower... I've always loved old churches.'

'St. Eutrope!'

'You see!'

They made their way slowly past enigmatic objects in a state of ruin, round which floated an odour of wax. Sometimes they met other visitors, attentive, learned, reverentially contemplating the exhibits; but these two had no thoughts for anyone but themselves.

'What did you say it was called?' asked Madeleine.

'The town? Saintes. It's not far from Royan.'

'I must have lived there once upon a time.'

'When you were a child, perhaps.'

'No,' said Madeleine calmly… 'In a former existence.'

Flavières couldn't bring himself to argue about it. Her words had raised too many echoes in himself.

'Where were you born?' he asked.

'In the Ardennes. Quite close to the frontier. Every war comes that way. And you?'

'I was brought up by a grandmother not far from Saumur.'

'I'm an only child,' said Madeleine. 'My mother was often ill. My father was away at the works all the time. It wasn't much fun.'

The next room was hung with pictures in glowing gilt frames. The portraits gazed at them fixedly, following them gravely with their eyes to the far end of the room—a nobleman with an emaciated face, a general smothered in gold lace, one hand on his sword, the other holding the bridle of a horse.

'When you were young,' asked Flavières softly, 'did you already have your… your dreams?'

'No. I was just a little girl like any other, except that I was very silent and reserved from being so much alone.'

'In that case… when did you start?'

'Quite suddenly, not very long ago… It seemed to me that I wasn't in my house, that I was living with a stranger. You know the feeling of waking up and not knowing where you are. It was rather like that.'

'There's another question I'd like to ask you, only I'm afraid you'd be angry.'

'I've no secrets,' answered Madeleine pensively.

'Can I?'

'Of course.'

'Do you ever think… of trying to… to disappear again?'

Madeleine stopped and looked at him with those eyes which always seemed to be beseeching someone.

'You haven't understood,' she murmured.

'That's no answer to my question.'

A small group of people were clustered in front of a picture. Flavières had a glimpse of a cross, a white body, the head hanging down over one shoulder, a trickle of blood under the left breast, a woman's face lifted towards the sky.

'You mustn't insist on an answer.'

'I do. I must. In your interest as well as mine.'

'Please… Roger…'

The words were spoken so quietly that he only just heard them, yet he was profoundly disturbed. He put his arm round her shoulders and drew her towards him, saying:

'Can't you see that I love you? I couldn't bear to lose you.'

They walked like two automatons between the Madonnas and Golgothas. She gave his hand a long squeeze.

'You frighten me,' he said, 'but I need you. Perhaps I need to be frightened… to teach me to despise my petty existence…'

'Let's go.'

They went through two empty rooms, looking for the way out. She was still hanging on to his arm, clinging more tightly than ever. They ran down some steps and found themselves, somewhat breathless, in front of a lawn in the middle of which a sprinkler was shedding a rainbow. Flavières stopped.

'I'm wondering whether we aren't both a little mad... Do you remember what I said to you just now?'

'Yes.'

'I told you I loved you. Did you hear that?'

'Yes.'

'If I told you so again, would you be angry?'

'No.'

'How extraordinary!... Shall we walk about a bit? We've got such a lot to say to each other.'

'No. I'm rather tired. I think I'll go home.'

She was pale and seemed afraid.

'I'll call a taxi,' suggested Flavières. 'Meanwhile, I want you to accept a little present.'

'What is it?'

'Open it and see. Go on. Open it.'

She undid the packet, slowly shaking her head. She saw the lighter and the cigarette-case. Opening the case she read the three words on the card.

'My poor friend,' she said.

'Come along.'

He dragged her into the Rue de Rivoli.

'I don't want you to thank me,' he said. 'I knew you needed a lighter... Shall we see each other tomorrow?'

She nodded her head.

'Good. We'll go into the country… No, no. Don't say any-thing. Leave me with the memory of this afternoon just as it is… Here's a taxi… *Eurydice chérie*… You don't know how happy you've made me.'

He seized her hand and kissed her gloved fingers.

'And stop looking back into the past,' he said, shutting the door on her.

He was tired out, with that peaceful exhaustion he had known as a boy when he had been running the whole day along the banks of the Loire.

FIVE

The whole morning Flavières had been waiting for Madeleine's telephone call. At two o'clock he was at their usual rendezvous at the Etoile. She didn't come. He rang Gévigne up at his office, only to be told he wouldn't be back from Le Havre till ten o'clock the following morning.

It was a horrible day, and the night was just as bad. He couldn't sleep. Well before dawn, he was up, wandering about in his room assailed by ghastly suppositions which he laboured to disprove. No. Nothing could have happened to Madeleine. It was impossible, unthinkable.

Yet he could think of nothing else!

He clenched his fists, trying to fight down the rising panic within him. Of course he'd been a fool: he should never have made that declaration to Madeleine. They had been disloyal to Gévigne, both of them. Who knew to what lengths remorse might not drive her, unstable as she was? As for him, he detested himself. For there was nothing with which he could reproach Gévigne. Gévigne had trusted him, had committed Madeleine to his care.

It was time to call off the whole stupid business. High time… But when Flavières tried to envisage life without Madeleine, he crumbled. His jaw dropped; he had to lean on his desk to prevent himself falling. He felt like hurling insults at God, destiny, the chance that had thrown her across his path, the occult powers—whatever they might be—which had woven this hideous tangle. He was doomed to be an outcast. The army had rejected him, and now…

He slumped down in the armchair Gévigne had sat in on that first visit. Wasn't he, Flavières, making rather heavy weather of it? Passion, a real passion, doesn't develop in a couple of weeks. With his chin in his hands, he looked coldly at himself. What did he know about love, he who had never yet loved anybody? Of course he had hankered after it, like a poor wretch gazing into a shop-window; he had, so to speak, made passes at it. But there had always been between the good things of life and himself a sort of hard, cold obstacle. And when he had entered the police it had seemed that he was now committed to the defence of all those things in the shop-window, which were thus, for him, more forbidden than ever. Madeleine was one of them. No, he had not the right to stretch out his hand. He couldn't pass into the camp of the thieves… All right, then. He must give her up… Coward! How could he ever enjoy his share of life if he knuckled under at the first hint of difficulty? Perhaps Madeleine was on the point of falling in love with him.

'Enough of this!' he said out loud. 'Enough of this! Why can't they leave me in peace?'

To dope himself, he made some strong coffee. From the kitchen he drifted back to his office, then back to the kitchen again. This strange new pain which gnawed at his entrails, constricted his chest making it difficult to breathe, and prevented him thinking clearly about anything, was the thing they called love. He felt himself ready to commit every extravagance and stupidity, and was almost proud of it in spite of his misery. How had he been able to receive that string of clients, study so many dossiers, and listen to so many confessions, without understanding this elemental thing, his mind obstinately closed to the truth? He had felt like shrugging his shoulders when a client, with tears in his eyes, had cried:

'But I love her!… I love her!'

He had felt like answering:

'Go on. You make me laugh with that stuff about love. Love indeed! A childish dream! Very pretty, no doubt, and exquisitely pure, but unrealistic. I'm just not interested in your bedroom stories!'

What a fool!

At eight o'clock he was still in his dressing-gown and slippers, his hair tousled, his eyes too bright. He hadn't made up his mind to any course of action. He couldn't telephone to Madeleine: she had forbidden him to, on account of the servants. Besides, what would be the use if she didn't want to see him? Perhaps she was afraid to…

He shaved and dressed, his thoughts elsewhere. Without it being in any way a conscious decision on his part, he knew he must see Gévigne as soon as possible. He suddenly wanted to be sincere, though at the same time making unavowed reservations. Why shouldn't he be able to find a way of reassuring Gévigne so that he could go on seeing Madeleine? That thought broke through the fog in which he was floundering.

With it, he noticed that the sun was shining outside, filtering in between the slats of the shutters, which he had forgotten to open. He switched off the electric light and flooded the room with sunshine. He was regaining confidence—just because it was a fine day, and because the war hadn't yet turned nasty. He went out, left the key under the mat for the charwoman, and, at the bottom of the stairs, greeted the concierge with an almost cheery 'good morning'. Yes, everything was going to turn out well after all. He could have laughed out loud at his qualms and terrors of an hour ago.

But then, he had always been like that, a prey to that mysterious inner pendulum which swung from despair to hope, from misery to joy, from timidity to audacity. No respite. Never a day of real relaxation, of moral equilibrium. Though with Madeleine…

No. He mustn't think of her, or he'd get all muddled again. To distract his attention he looked about him. Paris shimmered like a mirage; never had the light been more tender, more sensually palpable. One would have liked to touch the tree-tops, touch the sky, and take the whole magic city to one's bosom. Flavières went on foot, walking slowly. At ten sharp he entered Gévigne's office, to find that the latter had just arrived.

'Come in, old boy. Sit down… I'll be with you in a moment. I must just have a word with my Paris manager.'

Gévigne looked tired. In a few years he would have bags under his eyes, flabby, lined cheeks. He wouldn't get past fifty unscathed. Flavières couldn't help feeling secretly pleased. He had hardly settled down in his chair before Gévigne came back. He gave Flavières a friendly slap on the back as he passed.

'You know, I envy you,' he said. 'I'd just love to spend my afternoon escorting a pretty woman about the place—particularly if it was my own wife… The life I lead! It's no joke.'

He sat down heavily, swivelled his chair round, so as to face Flavières.

'Well?'

'Nothing. Nothing much. The day before yesterday we went to the Louvre. Yesterday I didn't see her. I was expecting her to ring me up, and I confess that her silence—'

'Nothing serious,' said Gévigne. 'Madeleine's been a little out of sorts. When I got back this morning I found her in bed. Tomorrow she'll be as right as rain again. I know her.'

'Did she speak about our afternoon in the Louvre?'

'She just mentioned it. She showed me some baubles she'd bought... a lighter, I think... She seemed all right to me.'

'I'm so glad.'

Flavières crossed his legs, threw an arm over the back of his chair. The sudden stab of relief was almost like a pain.

'You know, I'm wondering whether there's any use in my going on,' he said.

'What on earth are you saying? What an idea! You've seen for yourself what she's capable of doing.'

'Yes. Of course,' said Flavières awkwardly. 'But... Well, the thing is I'm beginning to find it a bit embarrassing going about with your wife. I look as if... Put it this way: it's an equivocal situation.'

Gévigne was fidgeting with a paper-knife.

'And what about me?' he growled. 'Do you think I like the situation any better? I appreciate your scruples, but we've no choice. If I had the time, I'd take on the job myself. But I've got myself so tied up...'

Dropping the paper-knife he folded his arms. His head seemed jammed down on his shoulders as he looked steadily at Flavières.

'Give me another fortnight, old man. Three weeks at the outside. Things are moving fast. I shall probably have to enlarge my shipyard and that'll mean settling down altogether at Le Havre. I hope Madeleine will agree to living there. Until then, keep an eye on her… I can see your point of view; I've given you both a delicate task and a thankless one. But don't chuck it up, I beg you. For the next two or three weeks I need to be free of all outside worries, so that I can concentrate on our new plans.'

Flavières made a pretence of hesitating.

'If you really think it's only a matter of two or three weeks.'

'You have my word for it.'

'All right. So long as you understand my position. I don't approve of these outings. I'm an impressionable type… You see, I'm being completely frank with you…'

Gévigne's face had a hard, businesslike look, the look he found useful at board meetings, no doubt. Yet, he smiled.

'Thank you,' he said. 'There aren't enough people in the world like you. I quite understand. But Madeleine's safety takes precedence over everything else.'

'Have you any particular reason for fearing anything?'

'No.'

'Has it occurred to you that if your wife acts on the spur of the moment, as she did the other day, I might not be able to intervene in time?'

'Yes… I've thought of… of everything.'

He lowered his eyes; he clenched a fist so tightly that his knuckles went white.

'But it won't happen,' he went on. 'And if it did, at least you'd be there to tell the tale. That would be something. What I can't bear is the uncertainty… I'd a hundred times sooner Madeleine was ill, desperately ill; I'd sooner she was undergoing the most dangerous operation. At least I should know where I was. *Bon*

75

dieu! I could count the chances one way or the other. But in this fog... Perhaps you don't understand that.'

'Oh yes, I do.'

'Then you'll carry on?'

'I will. Don't worry... By the way, do you know if she's ever been to Saintes?'

'Saintes?' exclaimed Gévigne, taken aback. 'No. I'm sure she hasn't. What put the idea into your head?'

'She described it exactly as if she'd been there.'

'What are you getting at now?'

'Would she have seen photographs of the town?'

'Anyone might see an old photograph of a place. That doesn't enable them to describe it. We've never been down the west coast. We haven't even got a guide-book of that region.'

'What about Pauline Lagerlac? Could she have lived there?'

'That's more than I could tell you.'

'It doesn't sound improbable... with a name ending in --*ac*. There are lots round there: Cognac, Chermignac, Germozac—oh, dozens of them.'

'And you think—'

'Of course I do. Your wife can describe places she's never seen herself, but which were known to Pauline Lagerlac... And, wait a minute. This is what's so interesting—she describes them not as they are now, but as they were a century ago.'

Gévigne frowned.

'How do you explain it?' he asked.

'I don't. I can't. Not yet. It's too extraordinary... Pauline and Madeleine...'

'But we're living in the twentieth century, you know! You're not going to pretend that Pauline and Madeleine... Of course I know that Madeleine is obsessed by this great-grandmother of hers, but there must be a reasonable explanation of it. That's why I turned to you. I was beginning to go off the rails a bit myself. I looked to you to steady me up, you with your legal mind.'

'I've offered to withdraw,' retorted Flavières, slightly nettled.

He was conscious of his own irritation, and realized how easily he and Gévigne could fly at each other's throats. But he wasn't ready to make peace.

'I won't waste your time any longer,' he said after a rather tense pause.

He got up. Gévigne merely shook his head.

'Come on, old man, we mustn't quarrel about it. All that matters is to save Madeleine. I don't care whether she's ill, mad, inspired, or possessed, so long as we can keep her alive.'

'Will she be going out today?'

'No.'

'When will she?'

'Tomorrow, surely. Today I'll try to be with her myself as much as possible.'

Flavières didn't wince though a spasm of hatred darted through him.

'How I loathe him!' he thought. 'How he disgusts me!'

Out loud he said:

'Tomorrow, then… That is if I'm free. I'm not so sure that I shall be.'

Gévigne jumped to his feet, came round and took Flavières' arm.

'I'm sorry if I've offended you,' he said. 'This business gets my nerves all jangled. I'm a bit tactless, I know, but it doesn't mean a thing… Listen. I've a particular reason for wanting you to look after her tomorrow. Today I'm going to sound her about moving to Le Havre. I've no idea how she'll take it. It may upset her. So be a sport. Keep tomorrow free at all costs. And in the evening give me a ring or drop in here. I've complete confidence in your judgment and am most grateful for all you're doing.'

Where had Gévigne learnt to speak in that grave, compelling voice so full of feeling?

'All right,' said Flavières.

Too promptly—he could have kicked himself. He was putting himself in Gévigne's power. But he had always been melted at once by a little solicitude, by a few kind words.

Ill at ease, he took his leave. As he went out, he heard Gévigne saying:

'I shan't forget what you're doing for me.'

And then the long hours began again, empty, monotonous, meaningless. He couldn't think of Madeleine now without thinking of Gévigne by her side, and each time he suffered the same rending, agonizing pain. He cursed himself. What sort of a man was he? He was letting Madeleine down as well as Gévigne. He was blind with jealousy, rage, envy, and despair. And yet, in the last resort, he felt himself to be both innocent and sincere. He had been straightforward throughout.

He dragged himself about, sometimes accusing, sometimes defending himself, sometimes so overwhelmed by depression that he had to sit down on a seat or at the terrace of a café. For he had another cross to bear now. What would become of him if Madeleine went to live at Le Havre? Should he try to stop her going? How could he?

He finished up in a cinema on the Grands Boulevards. The news was just beginning as he took his seat. Always the same subjects: marching troops, military parades, or manoeuvres. The people round him calmly sucked their sweets. Scenes of that sort were no longer of the slightest interest. Everybody knew that the Boches had had it! Flavières relapsed into an uneasy somnolence, like a forlorn traveller in a station waiting-room. He left before the end, afraid of falling asleep altogether. His neck was stiff, his eyes smarting. He dawdled home under a starry sky. Sometimes he passed a man in a steel helmet with a whistle lanyard round his neck, enjoying a furtive cigarette in a doorway. But a serious air raid seemed most unlikely. The Germans would need a really powerful air force for anything on a big scale, and that they simply hadn't got!

He lay down on his bed and lit a cigarette. And suddenly he felt so sleepy that he hadn't the energy to take his clothes off. His body went numb, petrified like those statues in the Louvre… Madeleine…

He woke up with a clear head, instantly recognizing the noise. Sirens. They howled in chorus over the roofs and the darkened city seemed like a hastily abandoned ship. In the house, a door slammed, then another. Steps hurried down the stairs. Flavières switched on his bedside lamp. Three o'clock. He turned over and went to sleep again.

At eight next morning he switched on the wireless with a yawn to hear the news. The German offensive had begun. And curiously enough he could only feel a sense of relief. Real war, at last. That would soon shake him out of his own personal troubles, making him share the general ones, which were both more exciting and more legitimate. Events would now take charge of things, making decisions for him which he shirked making for himself. Yes, the war was coming to his rescue. He had merely to let himself go, float down on the stream. A new spark of life kindled in him. He was hungry. His fatigue was gone. Madeleine rang up. The usual rendezvous. Two o'clock.

All the morning he worked briskly, saw clients, answered the telephone. He could detect in people's voices an excitement akin to his own. News was scarce. The papers and the radio made a lot of fuss over some initial successes, but without giving any precise details. That, of course, was only to be expected. He had lunch near the Palais de Justice with a colleague and they lingered over their coffee, talking. Everyone talked, even to strangers, discussing the situation, unfolding maps. Flavières enjoyed the free and easy atmosphere and the feeling of crisis, which he drank in with all his senses. He just had time to jump into his Simca and dash to the Etoile. He was drunk with words, with bustle, with sunshine.

Madeleine was waiting for him. Why had she chosen the same little brown suit she had worn the day she had…? For a moment Flavières retained her gloved hand in his.

'I nearly died of anxiety,' he said.

'I'm sorry. I wasn't very well. Can I drive?'

'By all means. I'm living on my nerves today. They're attacking. Have you heard?'

'Yes.'

She drove down the Avenue Victor-Hugo and Flavières realized at once she was still not quite herself. She changed gears clumsily, let the clutch in with a jerk, and jammed on the brakes. She had a bad colour.

'Let's go for a good long drive,' she said. 'It may be our last.'

'Why?'

She shrugged her shoulders.

'No one knows what's going to happen now. In any case I may be leaving Paris.'

So Gévigne had raised the question. Perhaps they'd had a row about it. Flavières didn't talk. He didn't want to take her mind off her driving till they were clear of the traffic. They left Paris by the Porte de la Muette and plunged into the Bois de Boulogne. Then he began:

'Why should you leave Paris? There's little risk of air raids, and this time the Germans won't even reach the Marne.'

When she didn't answer, he went on:

'Is it because of… because of me?… I don't want to disturb your life, Madeleine… You don't mind me calling you that now, do you?… All I want is that you promise never again to write a letter like that one you tore up… You understand what I mean?'

She pursed her lips, apparently intent on overtaking a lorry. The race-track at Longchamp looked like a huge meadow, and the eye instinctively looked for cows or sheep. There was a traffic jam at the Pont de Suresnes and for a while they only advanced at a walking pace.

'Don't let's talk about that any more,' she pleaded. 'And let's forget all about the war for a moment.'

'But you're sad, Madeleine. I can see you are.'

'Me?'

She made a brave attempt at a smile, which wrung his heart.

'No, I'm just the same as usual,' she went on. 'Really I am. I'm enjoying every moment of this drive. That's what I like— just to take whatever road turns up, without thinking about anything. I wish it was possible to stop thinking altogether. Oh, why aren't we animals?'

'You don't really mean that.'

'I do. I don't pity animals at all. On the contrary. They eat, they sleep, and they're innocent. They have no pasts and no futures.'

'Some philosophy, that!'

'I don't know whether it's a philosophy, but I can't help envying them.'

For the next hour they only exchanged an occasional remark. At Bougival they found the Seine again and followed the left bank for a while. A little later Flavières caught sight of the Château de Saint-Germain. In the deserted forest, Madeleine speeded up, only slowing down a little when they came to Poissy. Then she drove straight on, her eyes fixed on the road ahead. On the far side of Meulan a woman with a handcart full of logs was right in the middle of the road. Without waiting for her to pull over to the side, Madeleine turned down a lane to the right. They passed a makeshift saw-mill, which had been erected on the site for some job or other, and then abandoned. Only the smell of sawn timber told of its recent use. Coming to some cross-roads, Madeleine chose the righthand turning, presumably attracted by the hedges which were in full flower. A horse with a white spot on its forehead gazed at them over a five-barred gate.

Madeleine seemed to be in a hurry, though there was no reason for it, and the car bumped over the ruts. Furtively, Flavières looked at his wrist-watch. It was about time they stopped. Then they could walk together side by side. That would be the moment to question her. She was certainly hiding something. Possibly she had something on her conscience, something from long ago, perhaps before her marriage. Remorse could easily explain her obsession. She wasn't ill, she wasn't mad, she wasn't untruthful. Yet there might be something she had never been able to tell anybody, not even her husband. The more he thought of this idea, the more plausible he found it. But what could she be guilty of? For it would obviously be something serious.

'Do you know that church?' she asked. 'Have you any idea where we are?'

'What?... I'm sorry... That church?... No, I don't know where we are. Let's stop, anyhow. It's already half past three.'

They drew up in the empty square in front of the church. To one side, on a lower level, some roofs were visible behind a few trees.

'Queer mixture,' said Madeleine, looking critically at the church. 'Part Romanesque, part modern. It isn't good.'

'The tower's too tall for the rest.'

They went in. A notice over the stoup explained that the priest, having to minister to several other parishes, was only able to say one mass a week here, on Sundays at 11 a.m.

'That's why the place looks so neglected,' whispered Madeleine.

They went slowly on, between the rush-seated chairs. The clucking of hens came from a garden near by. The pictures of the stations of the cross were peeling. A wasp was buzzing round the altar. Madeleine crossed herself and knelt down on a dusty *prie-dieu*. Flavières stood by her, keeping very still. For what sin was she asking forgiveness? Would she have gone to hell if she had succeeded in drowning herself? Unable to hold out any longer, he knelt down beside her.

'Madeleine... Do you really believe?'

She turned her head slightly. She was so white he thought she was ill.

'What's the matter?… Tell me, Madeleine.'

'Nothing,' she whispered. 'Yes, I believe… I'm obliged to believe that nothing finishes when we think it does… That's what's so terrible.'

For a long minute she buried her face in her hands.

'Come on,' she said at last. 'Let's go.'

She stood up and crossed herself again, facing the altar. He plucked at her sleeve.

'Yes. We'd better go. I don't like to see you in this state.'

'I'll be all right outside in the fresh air.'

They passed a tumbledown confessional. Flavières was sorry he couldn't put Madeleine into it. That's what she needed: a priest. Priests forget. Would he forget, if she told her trouble to him? He heard her groping in the dim light for a latch. A door opened on a spiral staircase.

'That's the wrong door, Madeleine. It leads up into the belfry.'

'I'd like to have a look,' she answered.

'It's getting late.'

'I shan't be a minute.'

She had already started up the stairs. He couldn't very well stay behind. Reluctantly he followed, gripping the greasy rope which served as a banister rail.

'Don't go so quickly, Madeleine.'

His voice resounded in the narrow vaulted staircase. Madeleine took no notice; her steps hurried on. Reaching a little landing, he saw through an aperture the roof of the Simca, and, behind a screen of poplars, a field in which women were working, their hair bound in kerchiefs. Already at this height he felt uncomfortable and, hurriedly turning away from the loophole, he went on up the stairs.

'Madeleine!… Wait for me.'

He was panting and his temples were throbbing. Another landing, another loophole. This time he took care not to look. Nor on the other side either—that was worse. For the stairs swept round so as to leave an open shaft in the middle, down which hung the bell-rope. Rooks were cawing round the tower. He didn't know how he'd ever be able to get down again.

'Madeleine!'

His voice was hoarse with anxiety. Was he going to start yelling like a child in the dark? He was coming to another landing; he could see a glint of the light of the loophole. He knew very well what giddiness awaited him there: yet, when he got to it, he couldn't help looking. This time he was above the tree-tops and the Simca was no more than a little patch of black. The air came whistling in from everywhere, swirling round him. On the landing he found his further passage barred by a door. He tried to open it, but couldn't. He wasn't at the top. Looking across the bell-rope shaft he could see the stairs went on, though they were now encased, so there was no question of getting round the door that way.

'Madeleine!… Open the door.'

Frantically, he shook the handle and banged with his fist on the door. What was Madeleine up to? Could she be?…

'No, Madeleine!' he shouted wildly. 'You mustn't… Don't do that… Listen to me.'

His voice was picked up by the bells, which returned it with a slightly metallic resonance, a queer inhuman quality. Frantic, he turned towards the loophole. No, it was more than a loophole: on this landing it was quite a large aperture, divided in two by the door. Even the half was broad enough for a human body to squeeze through. Could a man pass the door that way, getting out one side and in the other? Yes, all the more so as there was a cornice on the level of the landing broad enough to offer a meagre foothold. Yes, it was possible… For a man!… Not for him! He'd fall: he knew it… No, he couldn't face it…

'Madeleine!' he shouted. 'Madeleine!'

She answered with a shrill cry and a shadow passed across the opening in the wall. Biting his knuckles he counted, as, when a boy, he had counted between the lightning and the thunder. And the thunder came—a horrid dull thud from below. In the voice of a dying man, Flavières repeated:

'Madeleine… Madeleine… No…'

He had to sit down. He felt he was going to faint. Then, without standing up, he lowered himself from step to step. It was a slow progress, and all the way he couldn't help groaning with terror and despair. On the first landing he risked a look. Kneeling, he peered out through the loophole. Beneath him, on the left, was an old churchyard, and straight below him, at the bottom of the horribly smooth wall, lay an ugly, shapeless heap of brown clothes. He wiped his eyes: he had to see at all costs. There was some blood on the gravel, a gaping black handbag from which a shining gold lighter had escaped.

Flavières wept. He didn't even think of going to her assistance. She was dead. And he was dead with her.

SIX

From a distance Flavières contemplated the body. He had come through the cemetery, but was now unable to advance another step. He remembered Madeleine's voice murmuring:

'It doesn't hurt to die.'

Desperately, he clung to that idea. No, she hadn't had time to suffer. They had said the same thing about Leriche. Like her, he had fallen head first. No time to suffer? Really? How could one be sure? When Leriche's head had smashed on the pavement, spattering blood all round...

Flavières couldn't finish the sentence. He had seen his companion's remains in the hospital; he had seen the doctor's report. And his fall had been from a lesser height than hers. He could imagine the terrible shock, a sort of explosion splintering the mind into little fragments... like a precious mirror reduced suddenly to atoms. Nothing was left of Madeleine now but that lifeless bundle made only of clothes, like a scarecrow.

He forced himself to come closer, obliging himself to look and to suffer, since he was responsible for everything. Through his tears he saw a blurred picture: her hair had come undone and to that faint mahogany tint was now added streaks of blood, a hand was already wax-like, her wedding ring glittered on one of the fingers. If he had dared, he would have taken that ring and worn it on his little finger. Instead he merely picked up the lighter.

Poor little Eurydice! She would never come back from the nothingness into which she had plunged.

He backed slowly away, still staring at her as though he had killed her himself. He was suddenly frightened of this horrible heap, across which flitted the occasional shadow of a rook. He fled. Hurrying between the gravestones, his fingers tightly clenched on the lighter, it suddenly occurred to him that it was in a cemetery that he had first studied Madeleine, and it was in a cemetery again that he was taking leave of her.

It was all over. No one would ever know why she had killed herself. No one would ever know he had been there, or that he had not had the courage to get beyond that door. He made his way round to the front of the church and took refuge in his car. His reflection in the windscreen filled him with disgust. He hated himself for being alive—if you could call it that. It was more like being in hell.

He drove for a considerable time without knowing where he was. Then, to his amazement, he recognized the station of Pontoise. In the town he passed the *gendarmerie*. Ought he to go in and raise the alarm? Ought he to give himself up? No. He had committed no fault in the eyes of the law. They would merely think him insane. What could he do, then? Put a bullet through his brain? Impossible: he'd never have the guts. More than ever now, he had to live with the knowledge that he was a coward. He had no head for heights! Rubbish. That was no excuse. It was willpower he lacked. Ah! How right Madeleine had been! Far better be an animal! To graze peacefully till it was time for the pole-axe!

It was six o'clock when he entered Paris by the Porte d'Asnières. Of course, he had to tell Gévigne: there was no avoiding that. He stopped at a café in the Boulevard Malesherbes. He washed his face and brushed his hair, then went into the telephone-box. A voice he didn't know informed him that Gévigne was out and not expected back at the office that day. He drank a glass of brandy, standing at the bar. Grief pervaded him like a sort of drunkenness. He had the impression he was living in an aquarium, that other people swam past him noiselessly as fish. He had another brandy. Every now and again he would tell himself that Madeleine was dead. He wasn't surprised—not really. How could he be? Hadn't it been obvious all along that he would lose her in this way? He would have had to pour out far more vitality than he possessed to keep her in this world.

'*Garçon, la même chose.*'

Yes, he needed yet another. He had saved her once. That was something, wasn't it? He really had no right to reproach himself. Even if he had got past that door, he would have been too late to stop her. She was too set on dying. Gévigne had chosen the wrong man for the job—that was the long and short of it. He should have chosen someone very charming, brilliant—an artist perhaps—but in any case someone brimming over with energy and gaiety. He had chosen a niggling type, too preoccupied with himself, a prisoner of his own past… But what was the good?… The damage was done now…

Flavières paid for his drinks and went. God, he was tired! He drove slowly to the Etoile. A few hours ago she had held that wheel he was holding now. He envied those clairvoyants who, from merely holding a handkerchief or an envelope, could read a person's most secret thoughts. How dearly he would have liked to know the last agony of Madeleine's mind. No, that was putting it badly—there hadn't been any agony. It was her indifference to life—that was the real secret. She had walked out of it without a qualm. She had plunged head first, her arms wide open, welcoming the earth that was about to kill her. It wasn't so much that she was escaping this life, she was going *back* to something, going home…

It had been a mistake to drink all that brandy. His thoughts were all over the place. He turned into the Avenue Kléber and parked the Simca behind Gévigne's big black car. He was no longer afraid of Gévigne. This was the last time he'd see him. He walked up the stairs, rather too ceremonial with their red carpet and white stone. Gévigne's brass name-plate was on a double door. Flavières rang. He took his hat off before the door was open and stood waiting humbly.

'Monsieur Gévigne?… Maître Flavières.'

Madeleine's home! He tried to put a special meaning into his eyes as they roamed over the furniture, the curtains, the ornaments. He was saying good-bye. The pictures in the *salon* were disturbing in their strangeness. They were mostly of animals—unicorns, swans, birds of paradise, which were painted in a way which recalled Douanier Rousseau. Flavières went up to one of them and read the signature: *Mad. Gév.* Was it these fantastic creatures that were now welcoming her in the other world? Where had she seen that black lake, those water-lilies like chalices full of poison, that forest of tree-trunks and lianas which stood solemnly watching a dance of humming-birds? Over the mantelpiece was the portrait of a young woman round whose slender neck was an amber necklace. Pauline Lagerlac. Her hair was done just like Madeleine's. The face, tortured without being distorted, had an absent expression as if the soul was at grip with some problem known to her alone.

Profoundly troubled, Flavières stood gazing at it till the door opened behind him.

'You at last!' said Gévigne.

Flavières turned round and managed to find just the right tone of voice in which to say:

'Is she here?'

'What?… It's you who ought to know where she is.'

Flavières sank into an easy chair. He didn't have to do any play-acting to look distraught.

'We didn't go out together today,' he explained. 'I waited for her at the Etoile up to four o'clock… Then I went to the hotel in the Rue des Saints-Pères, to the Passy Cemetery, anywhere where I thought I had a chance of finding her… I've just got back… And, if she's not here…'

He looked up at Gévigne, who had gone quite white. His eyes were staring, his mouth open, like a man being strangled.

'No, Roger,' he stammered. 'You're not… You're not telling me… You can't be…'

Flavières opened his hands.

'I tell you I've looked everywhere.'

'It's impossible… Do you realize that…'

He tapped with his foot on the carpet, wrung his hands, then flopped down in a corner of a sofa.

'We must find her,' he gasped. 'We must find her at once… At once… I couldn't bear it if…'

He thumped the arm of the sofa with all his might, and there was in that reflex such rage, such suffering, and such violence that it reacted on Flavières who began to get angry, too.

'When a woman's made up her mind to run away,' he said spitefully, 'it's pretty hard to stop her.'

'Run away? Run away? As if Madeleine was a woman to run away! I only wish I could think it possible… By now she may well be…'

He jumped up, almost knocking over a small table. He walked to the far end of the room. With his shoulders hunched and his head forward, he looked like a wary boxer.

'What does one do in a case like this?' he asked. 'You ought to know. Does one call in the police?… For heaven's sake say something, man!'

'They'd laugh in our faces. If she'd been gone two or three days, it would be a different matter.'

'Not if it came from you. They know you… And if you explained that Madeleine had already tried to kill herself, that you'd dragged her out of the Seine with your own hands, and that she might well have tried again today, they'd believe you, I'm sure…'

'We've nothing to go on, old chap. She's been out a few hours. She'll be back for dinner—you'll see.'

'Supposing she's not?'

'In any case it's not my business to report her missing.'

'So you wash your hands of it?'

'It's not that… Try and understand… It's the normal thing for the husband to call in the police.'

'All right, I'll do so at once.'

'You'd only be making a fool of yourself. In any case they wouldn't take any action on such flimsy evidence. They'd merely take down the particulars and promise to let you know if she turned up. That's all. I know.'

Slowly Gévigne put his hands in his pockets.

'If I have to sit here and wait, I'll go out of my mind.'

He began pacing up and down, then stopped in front of a bowl of roses on the mantelpiece, which he contemplated mournfully.

'I must be going now,' said Flavières.

Gévigne didn't budge. He went on looking at the flowers. Only a slight tremor passed over his face.

'In your place,' went on Flavières hurriedly, 'I'd simply put the thing out of my mind. It's only just gone seven. She might have lingered in a shop, or met someone.'

'You just don't care,' snarled Gévigne. 'Why should you?'

'There's absolutely no need to get all worked up about it. If she's run away, she can't have got far.'

He explained politely to Gévigne the various methods employed by the police to track down missing persons. He warmed up to the subject in spite of his exhaustion. He seemed to have become two people at once. One was eagerly proving that Madeleine couldn't escape, and almost proving it to himself. The other would have liked to fling himself down on the carpet and sob out his heart's despair. Still gazing at the flowers, Gévigne seemed completely lost in thought.

'Give me a ring when she comes in,' said Flavières, making for the door.

Yes, it was high time he went. He could no longer control his features, no longer trust his eyes. The truth was surging up within him. At any moment he might burst out:

'She's dead... Madeleine's dead.'

'Don't go,' muttered Gévigne.

'I must. I'd stay if I could, of course. But if you knew how my work was piling up...'

'Don't go,' pleaded Gévigne again. 'I couldn't bear to be alone when they... when they bring her back.'

'Come on, Paul. You're losing your sense of proportion.'

Gévigne's immobility was positively frightening.

'If you're here, you can explain to them all we've done, the struggle we've had…'

'Of course… But no one's going to bring her back. Take my word for it.'

Flavières' voice had faltered. To gain time, he whipped out his handkerchief, coughed, blew his nose.

'Keep your chin up, Paul… It'll all come right… Don't forget to give me a ring.'

As he opened the door he looked back. With his head sunk on his chin, Gévigne seemed turned to stone. Flavières went out, shutting the door gently behind him. He crossed the hall on tip-toe. He felt sick with disgust, and yet relieved. The hardest part was over. The Gévigne Case was wound up. As for what Gévigne was suffering… But wasn't he, Flavières, suffering just as much? More! He had to admit, as he got into his car and slammed the door, that he had almost from the first regarded himself as Madeleine's real husband. Gévigne was only a usurper. And you don't sacrifice yourself for a usurper; you don't go to the police, to your former colleagues, and explain to them that you've allowed a young woman to kill herself because you hadn't the courage to go to her rescue… You don't for the second time in your life accept dishonour for the sake of a man who… No. Leave that alone! Silence! Peace! The thing now was to get away, and did not that client of his at Orléans provide an excellent pretext for leaving Paris?

Flavières never knew how he managed to drive back to the garage. He was walking now, not caring where he went, down a street bathed in an evening light which seemed to float in straight from the country, very blue, sad, and with overtones of war. At a crossing there was a crowd pressing round a car which had two mattresses lashed down on the roof. The world was becoming chaotic. As darkness fell all lights were extinguished, and the subdued crowd ebbed back into their homes leaving deserted squares whose silence tore at one's heart. Everything conspired to bring his mind back to the dead woman. He entered a small restaurant in the Rue Saint-Honoré and chose a table in the far corner.

'*A la carte*?' asked the waiter.

'No, I'll have the *table d'hôte*.'

He couldn't bear to choose, yet he must eat something. He must try to go on living as before. He thrust his hand in his pocket to touch the lighter, and Madeleine's face sprang up before him, floating between his eyes and the white tablecloth.

'She never loved me,' he mused. 'She never loved anybody.'

He swallowed his soup mechanically. He was detached from the things of the world, like an ascetic. He would live henceforth as a pauper, wallowing in his grief, imposing penances to punish himself. He might even buy a whip and take to flagellation. It was only right he should hate himself. He must hate himself for a long time before he had a right to any self-respect.

'They've broken through at Liège,' said the waiter. 'Seems the Belgians are falling back, just as they did in '14.'

'Gossip,' said Flavières. 'Pay no attention to it.'

Liège was a long way off, right up at the top of the map. What happened up there had nothing to do with Flavières. In any case, this war they talked so much about was only a tiny episode in the death-struggle which was his.

'On the Place de la Concorde one of our customers saw a car that was fairly riddled with bullets.'

'The next course, please,' said Flavières.

Why couldn't they leave him alone? Belgians! Why not Dutchmen? Silly ass! He hurried over the meat. It was tough, but he didn't complain, since he had resolved never to complain again. He would accept anything. What was painful would be grist to his mill. With the fruit, however, he drank two glasses of brandy, and his thoughts began to emerge from the fog in which they had been floundering for the last few hours. His elbows on the table, he lit a cigarette. With the lighter, of course, and that gave the smoke he inhaled something of the substance of Madeleine. He tasted her, retained her for a moment within him.

He was certain now that Madeleine hadn't done anything wrong before her marriage. It was a stupid supposition. Gévigne would have made enquiries: he wasn't the man to buy a pig in a poke. Another thing: Madeleine's remorse would have been inexplicably tardy, since for several years she had appeared quite normal. The trouble had started at the beginning of February—there was no getting away from that.

Flavières pressed on the spring of the lighter, and watched the thin tongue of flame for a moment before blowing it out. The metal was warm in his hand. No, Madeleine's motives were not everyday ones. He had approached the problem too crudely, trying to boil everything down to simple cause and effect. He wouldn't make that mistake again: he would purify himself, cauterize himself with red-hot needles, until one day he would be worthy to fathom the mystery of Pauline Lagerlac. In the end it would no doubt come to him in a flash. He pictured himself a monk, kneeling down on the beaten earth which formed the floor of his cell; but it was not a crucifix to which he raised his eyes, but Madeleine's photograph, the one he had seen on Gévigne's desk.

He rubbed his eyes, wiped his forehead, and asked for the bill. Hell! They knew how to sting you in this place!... Never mind. No recriminations. They weren't allowed: it was part of the punishment. He went out. It was quite dark now, except for a narrow band of stars between the tall houses. Sometimes a car passed, its lights dimmed and shaded. Flavières couldn't make up his mind to go home. He dreaded the telephone call which told him the body had been found. And he wasn't sorry to impose still more fatigue on this body of his which he held responsible for such a catastrophe. He walked at random in a sort of dizzy abandon. He would keep watch till dawn. It was a question of dignity. Of something else, too: where Madeleine had gone she might be in need of a friendly thought. Little Eurydice!

Tears welled up into his eyes. He tried hard to form as it were a concrete picture of nothingness, so that he could keep her company at least for her first night there. The nearest he could get to it was Paris in the black-out, and he had to make the best of that. Yes, it was good to wander through those shadows. The land of the living was far away. Here were only the dead, solitary figures slinking through the streets, haunted by the bright days of long ago, tortured by a remembered happiness. Some stopped for a moment to look down at the dark river licking its banks, then slunk on again. Were they preparing themselves for the Day of Judgment? What was it the waiter had said?

'They've broken through at Liège.'

Flavières sat down on one of the seats on the quay, and threw his arms over the back. Tomorrow he'd go away... His head swayed; he shut his eyes; he had just time to formulate the thought:

'You're going to sleep after all. Shirker!'

He slept with his mouth wide open like a tramp spending the night on a bench in a police station. It was much later when he was woken up by the cold. He groaned. He had cramp in his right leg, and walked away, limping in the bleak daylight of early morning. Shivering and with a parched mouth, he felt ghastly, and took refuge in a café that was just opening. The wireless was blaring away, announcing that the situation was confused and that the infantry were engaged in plugging up a few breaches. He ate a couple of *croissants* dipped into his coffee, and took the Metro home.

He had hardly shut his door when the telephone rang.

'Hallo! Is that you, Roger?'

'Yes.'

'I was right, you know. She's killed herself.'

It was better to say nothing. He stood listening uncomfortably to Gévigne's breathing. He seemed to be blowing right into Flavières' ear.

'I was told last night,' he went on at last. 'An old woman found her at the foot of a church tower at Saint-Nicolas.'

'Where's that?'

'North of Mantes... A little village of nothing at all between Sailly and Drocourt... I can't take it in.'

'What was she doing out there?'

'Wait a minute. I'd better tell you everything. She threw

herself from the top of the tower and crashed in the churchyard. The body was taken to the hospital at Mantes.'

'Poor chap. It's awful for you. Are you going?'

'I've just come back. Of course I went immediately. I tried to get hold of you, but you weren't in. I've got a few urgent things to see to, then I'm going back to Mantes again. The police have started an enquiry.'

'They're bound to, though it's obviously suicide.'

'They're puzzled about one or two things, why she should have come so far to do it, for instance. I don't know how much to tell them. I don't want it known that Madeleine…'

'They won't look very far.'

'All the same, I'd have liked you to be with me.'

'Out of the question I'm afraid. I've got a big case at Orléans to see to. I simply can't put it off any longer.'

'Will you be away long?'

'Oh no. Only a couple of days. And I'm sure you won't need me.'

'I'll give you another ring… I'd have liked you to be at the funeral.'

Gévigne was still breathing as though he'd been running.

'My dear Paul,' said Flavières with genuine feeling, 'I'm terribly sorry.'

He lowered his voice to ask:

'She wasn't too badly…?'

'Not her face… Her poor face! If you'd seen it!'

'Hold tight, old man. I know how you feel. So do I.'

He rang off. Steadying himself with a hand against the wall, he tottered to his bed.

'So do I,' he said, choking. 'So do I.'

And he dropped like a stone into deep sleep.

Next day he took the first train to Orléans. He couldn't face the idea of driving. News from the front was by no means reassuring, however much it might try to be. In enormous headlines people could read: *German Offensive Contained* or *Fierce Fighting Round Liège*, but details were sadly lacking, the tone of articles was evasive, and people affected an optimism which ill-concealed their gnawing anxiety.

Flavières dozed in his corner. Outwardly he looked himself: inwardly he was ravaged, corroded, burnt-out, and blackened, his four walls left standing round a heap of wreckage. With that picture he nourished his misery, making it more bearable. He was beginning to respect his ordeal.

At Orléans he took a room in a hotel opposite the station. It was when he went out to buy some cigarettes that he saw the first car-load of refugees, a huge Buick loaded with luggage covered with dust. Some women were asleep inside. He went to see his client, but the conversation didn't get much farther than the war. At the Palais de Justice it was being whispered that Corap's army was retreating. The Belgians were blamed: accused of losing their heads. The older men recalled the time when for three whole days Parisians had heard the distant rumble of the guns on the Marne.

Flavières found Orléans agreeable. In the evenings he wandered along the quays watching the swallows skimming over the mauve water of the Loire. On the terraces of the cafés, people seemed all to be nursing the same secret, while the advancing summer made the long twilights pathetically lovely. What was going on in Paris? Was Madeleine buried yet? Had Gévigne returned to his shipyard at Le Havre? Flavières sometimes raised such questions, cautiously, like a convalescent lifting the bandage to have a peep at his wound. Of course, he still suffered, but the hideous agony of the first days had given way to a chilly numbness that was occasionally pierced by a sharp stab of remembrance.

It was known now that German armour was advancing on Arras, and that the fate of the country was in the balance. Every day more cars drove through the town, looking for the bridge and the road to the South. And people stood in the streets silently staring at them, their hearts empty. They were more and more dirty, more and more ramshackle. With a shamefaced curiosity, people would question the fugitives. In all this, Flavières saw the image of his own disaster. He had no longer the strength to go back to Paris.

His eyes fell on the article by chance. He was listlessly scanning the newspaper as he sipped his coffee. The headline was on the fourth page. The police were enquiring into Madeleine's death, were questioning Gévigne. It was so incongruous after the news on the front page with the photographs of villages in ruins. He read the article right through a second time. The police seemed to have ruled out the possibility of suicide. That just showed how much use the police were, playing with fancy theories while the roads were chock-a-block with refugees! He, at any rate, knew the truth, and as soon as the situation improved he'd go and tell them Gévigne was innocent. For the moment, trains ran very irregularly.

Other days followed, and the newspapers devoted all their space to the chaotic battle which was devastating the plains of the North. No one knew who was where: Germans, French, English, and Belgians seemed all mixed up in an inextricable tangle. Flavières thought less and less often of Gévigne. All the same, he fully intended to straighten out the muddle at the first opportunity. That decision enabled him to regain some of his self-esteem, and allowed him to share a little more the emotions of his fellow men. He went to a mass at the Cathedral in honour of Joan of Arc, and prayed for France and Madeleine at the same time. He made little distinction now between the national disaster and his own. France was Madeleine lying crushed and bleeding at the foot of a church tower.

And then one morning the inhabitants of Orléans in their turn began to load up their cars. Flavières' client was one of the first to disappear.

'Why don't you go south, too?' said one of his friends. 'There's nothing to keep you here.'

With a sudden spurt of courage he tried to ring Gévigne up. No answer. The station at Saint-Pierre-des-Corps was bombed. With death in his soul, Flavières boarded a motor-coach bound for Toulouse. Little did he realize he was leaving for four years.

PART TWO

ONE

'Take a deep breath... Cough... Another deep breath... Fine... As for the heart... Hold your breath a moment... Hum!... Not so good... You can put your clothes on again.'

The doctor looked at Flavières, who put on his shirt, then turned away a little awkwardly to do up his fly-buttons.

'Married?'

'No... I've just come back from Africa.'

'Were you a prisoner?'

'No. I was called up in 1940, but the doctors wouldn't pass me. It was my lungs, I believe. The result of a pleurisy I'd had two years before.'

'Are you thinking of living here in Paris?'

'I don't know. I've got a practice at Dakar, but I might go back to my former one here.'

'Lawyer?'

'Yes. The trouble is, my flat's been taken over by somebody else. And to find a place these days...'

The doctor scratched an ear, still studying Flavières, who was fumbling irritably with his tie.

'You drink, don't you?'

Flavières shrugged his shoulders, but his face had fallen.

'Do you mean you can see signs of it?'

'It's your affair, of course,' said the doctor.

'Yes, I drink a bit,' Flavières admitted. 'Life's not that beautiful.'

It was the doctor's turn to shrug his shoulders. He sat down at his desk and removed the cap of his fountain pen.

'Your general condition is far from satisfactory,' he observed. 'You need a good rest. In your place, I'd settle somewhere in the Midi—at Nice for instance, or Cannes… As for the obsessions you've told me about, they're not within my field. You must see a specialist about that. I'm giving you a note for my colleague, Dr. Ballard.'

'In your opinion,' muttered Flavières, 'is it serious?'

'Go and see Ballard.'

His pen scratched over the paper. Flavières took out his wallet and produced some notes.

'Go to the Food Office,' said the doctor, still writing. 'With this certificate you'll be given an extra ration of meat and fats. But what you need most is warmth and rest. Avoid all worries. No correspondence, and no reading… It's three hundred francs… Thanks.'

He was already conducting Flavières to the door while a fresh patient came in through another. Flavières went down the stairs, grumbling. A specialist! A psychiatrist who would unearth all his secrets, would make him talk about Madeleine's death. Out of the question! Rather than that, he would go on living with his nightmares, losing himself every night in a labyrinth of corridors crawling with vermin, or searching frantically for someone in the dark. It was the heat of Dakar and the glaring light that had got him down. Now he was saved.

He turned up his coat-collar and started towards the Place des Ternes. He hardly recognized this Paris, still plunged in the mists of winter, these great empty spaces, these broad avenues along which hardly anything passed but bicycles and jeeps.

He felt a little out of place, being too well dressed. He hurried along quickly like everyone else. The Arc de Triomphe loomed up indistinctly in the grey mist. Everything was the colour of the past, the colour of memory. What feast of the dead had he come here to celebrate? Wouldn't he have done better to have stayed where he was? What did he expect from this pilgrimage? He had known other women: the old wound was healed. So, at least, he had thought.

He went into *Dupont's* and chose a seat near the window. A few officers, lost in the immense round room. Except for the hissing of the percolator, dead silence. A sulky waiter looked him up and down, studying the cloth his overcoat was made of, his crêpe-soled suede shoes.

'A cognac,' said Flavières, 'and mind it's a real one.'

He knew how to rap out his words in a café or restaurant. He possessed authority, perhaps because of the intense passion which ravaged his face. He put down the brandy at a single gulp.

'Not bad,' he muttered. 'Give me another.'

He threw some money on the table. That was another habit he'd acquired at Dakar. He handled the crumpled notes with an off-hand air, as though he had returned from the ends of the earth, as though all men owed him a debt which they would never be able to pay.

With his arms folded, he contemplated the yellow liquor which was so cunningly able to reawaken the phantoms. No, Madeleine wasn't dead. From the moment he had stepped down on to the station platform she had never left him alone. There are faces which you forget. They get worn down gradually by the wind and the rain till the features are lost in vagueness, like the figures of stone round the doorway of a cathedral.

She would never be like that: her image was intact, and he could see the afternoon sunshine round her, glowing like a halo. The final image of her, the horrid bloody one, had been effaced. If it ever tried to intrude, it was easily pushed back again. The others, all of them, were miraculously fresh, animated, engaging.

His hand closed round the glass, Flavières sat absolutely motionless. He could feel the warmth of early May, could see streams of cars sweeping round the Arc de Triomphe. And she came, her bag tucked under her arm, her eyes shadowed as though made up by her little veil... She leant over the parapet of the bridge and dropped the red tulip... She tore the letter into little bits which she scattered in the wind...

Flavières drank his cognac. He felt old now. What had he got to look forward to? Solitude and illness!... While the other survivors of the war were busy gathering together their bits and pieces, rebuilding their homes, renewing their friendships, in short, reconstituting the future, he had nothing but ashes to poke... So why should he give up the one thing which...

'Waiter! The same again.'

He would limit himself to that. He didn't really like alcohol. He only took it to rekindle the embers deep down within him, making them give out a faint glow of hope. When he went out, the cold air made him cough, but Paris was no longer hostile to him. He reached the Etoile and for a moment stood on the kerb pretending he was waiting for her. The fine misty drizzle floated past him, but she didn't come. She never would. Gévigne had perhaps left Paris, too. Flavières turned into the Avenue Kléber and looked for the house. The shutters on the second floor were closed. The Talbot had no doubt been requisitioned for some general. What about the pictures? Would they still be up there, the dreamy girl over the mantelpiece, the birds of paradise?… When he went in he found the concierge sweeping the hall.

'Monsieur Gévigne, please.'

'Monsieur Gévigne?'

She stared blankly at Flavières, then said:

'He's been dead a long time, poor man.'

'Paul! Dead!' muttered Flavières.

What was the good of going on? That's what he would find all along the line. Death, death, nothing but death!

'Come in, won't you?' said the concierge.

She shook out her broom and opened the door of her lodge.

'I left in '40,' said Flavières.

'Ah! That explains it.'

By the window was an old man with steel-rimmed glasses who had one hand in a shoe, which he was thoughtfully examining. He looked up.

'Don't let me disturb you,' said Flavières.

'You can't even buy a bit of cardboard to mend a shoe with,' grumbled the old man.

'Were you a friend of Monsieur Gévigne's?' asked the concierge.

'A very old one. He rang me up to tell me of his wife's death. But I had to leave Paris that very day.'

'Poor man. He couldn't bear to go back there alone, and, as there was nobody else, I went with him myself. And it was I who laid her out and dressed her, for, as you can imagine…'

Flavières longed to ask her in what clothes she dressed Madeleine. The grey suit perhaps…

'Sit down,' said the concierge. 'I expect you've got a minute to spare.'

'Thank you… I did hear that the police were bothering him.'

'Bothering him! I should think they were. It was touch and go whether they arrested him or not.'

'But that's absurd. I thought she committed suicide.'

'Of course she did. But you know what the police are… He had enemies—people who envied him his money… And when the police start rummaging in a man's past… I couldn't tell you how many times they came here. As for the questions they asked! About him… About his wife… Did they get on together?… Was he here the day it happened?… On and on till you hardly knew what you were saying… Do you remember, Charles?'

The old man, with the aid of a kitchen knife, was cutting out a sole from the lid of a box.

'Yes,' he growled, 'it was a pretty mess. Like it is now.'

'But how did he die—Monsieur Gévigne?'

'He was killed on the road, near Le Mans. One morning he came down in a great state. "I have had enough of this," he said. "I'm clearing out, and if they want me they can damned well come and fetch me." He'd known us a long time, you see, and always spoke his mind… So he threw a few bits of luggage into his car, and off he went… We heard afterwards… machine-gunned. He died while they were carrying him to the hospital… It's a shame…'

'If I'd been there,' thought Flavières, 'he wouldn't have had to clear out. The plane would have machine-gunned someone else. Some unknown person. Anyhow, not him. And I should have been able to talk to him now and explain to him…'

He wrung his hands. He ought never to have come back.

'Fate was against them, poor things,' went on the concierge. 'Yet they got on very well together.'

'Wasn't she a bit… a bit odd?'

'Not in the least… She always looked rather sad, particularly in those dark clothes she wore, but it was just her nature… And she was always so happy when she could go out with him.'

'Which wasn't often,' sneered the old man.

She rounded on him.

'With things as they were, he never had the time. Always having to rush to and fro between Paris and Le Havre. You can't deny it.'

'Where's she buried?'

'At Saint-Ouen. And misfortune pursued her even there. When the Americans bombed La Chapelle, all that part of the cemetery which touches the railway was properly churned up. Bones lying about everywhere, mixed up with fragments of gravestones. I think they held a service there and buried the bones again.'

Flavières trembled in his overcoat, the collar of which concealed half his face.

'Her grave?' he just managed to ask.

'Same as the others. Nothing left of it. They've filled up the holes in the ground—craters they call them—and tidied the place up, but that's all they've been able to do as yet.'

'No need to pity the dead,' grunted the old man. 'They're better off than we are.'

Flavières pushed back the horrible images which rose to his mind. He felt the bitter impotence of tears that would not flow. More than ever now, it was finished: the page was turned.

Madeleine was annihilated. In antique manner she had had her funeral pyre—of T.N.T.—and her ashes had been scattered by the blast. That face which came to haunt him was now nothing, nothing at all. He must push it back into the shades where it belonged, and try to live…

'The flat?'

'Shut up for the moment… Some kind of cousin of hers has inherited the building… It's all very sad.'

'Yes,' murmured Flavières, 'it's very sad.'

He picked up his hat and rose to his feet.

'It's a shock, I know,' said the concierge, 'when you suddenly hear of the death of an old friend.'

The old man began nailing on the new sole, the blows of his hammer making ugly thumps. Flavières almost ran into the street, where the drizzle deposited a slimy film on his face. He could feel the fever once more, rising in his arteries. Crossing the road, he sat down in the little café where he had once filled in the time, waiting for Madeleine.

'Give me something strong.'

'You look as if you needed it.'

The man looked round, then lowered his voice to ask:

'A little whisky?'

Flavières lolled against the bar. A glow of warmth was spreading through his chest. His grief was melting like a lump of ice, was changing into a calm melancholy.

The doctor was right, of course. He had to go slow; he needed sunshine and an easy mind. That was the most important thing of all—an easy mind. He mustn't think of Madeleine. He had meant, in coming to Paris, to visit her grave. She no longer had one. That was all to the good: the last link was broken.

His pilgrimage had come to an end, here in this little *bistrot* in front of a glass of sunny yellow liquor. All that he had loved, the vagrant spirit, the gentle stranger he had dragged back from the shadows that lured her, all led up to this glass of whisky in which it was now to dissolve.

Perhaps the whole story had been a dream, conceived in a moment of exaltation. No, it couldn't be: he still had the lighter. He put a cigarette between his lips, took the gold lighter from his pocket. For a second or two he weighed it in the hollow of his hand. Should he throw it away? Or if he hadn't the courage for that, he might merely lose it, like a dog one hasn't the heart to destroy. Perhaps, but later on. For the moment...

He had just made a decision, succumbed rather to one that had been made for him, as always. He put down his empty glass and paid royally. He liked to see faces light up with a servile joy.

'Is it possible to get a taxi?'

'Hum! It's not easy. How far do you want to go?'

'Near Mantes.'

'Gracious! Still, I'll see what I can do.'

Smiling all the time at Flavières, he put through three telephone calls. After the last, he said:

'Gustave'll take you. It may be a bit expensive, of course. With the price of petrol on the black market...'

The taxi, an old bone-shaker, was there in no time. Before leaving, Flavières stood drinks all round. He had no scruples when he had an aim in view. He explained carefully to Gustave:

'We're going to a little place north of Mantes. Between Sailly and Drocourt there's a tiny village... But I'll show you the way... I shan't be there long...'

They drove off. The wintry roads told a mournful story of

skirmishes, battles, and bombings. Chilled to the bone, Flavières sat huddled in his corner, watching the black fields sweep past, trying to conjure up pictures of budding trees and beds of white flowers. In vain. Madeleine was slipping away from him: she was beginning really to die. Come on! Another effort!

He knew very well he had never been really in love. He had never seen himself with such clarity as now. He had taken to drink just to silence this sceptical, sneering observer who liked to knock the bottom out of every illusion, who accused him of deluding himself with storybook stuff, of reciting to himself an interminable elegy to gratify his taste for melancholy, solitude, and impotence. Only, it needed always more and more drink to banish this cynical debunker. Only when several glasses had spread their numbing warmth through his brain could Madeleine reappear, gentle and merciful. She spoke to him of the life that might have been, and he glowed with happiness. But it was the other Flavières who woke up next morning with his mouth full of bitter, insulting words.

'Here's Sailly,' cried Gustave.

With his fingers, Flavières cleared a space on the misty window.

'Turn right at the next crossing. Then it'll be two or three kilometres.'

The taxi rattled along a lane full of ruts and potholes. Drips from the wet trees, blackened by the rain, fell on to the dead leaves in the ditches. Now and again a house slipped by, a wisp of blue smoke rising from the chimney.

'There's a church ahead,' said Gustave.

'With a tall tower? That's the place.'

The car drew up in front of the church, just as the Simca had done long ago. Flavières got out and looked up at the cornice which ran round the tower. He wasn't moved. But he had never felt colder in his life. He went off to find the houses whose roofs he had seen from the tower. There they were, huddled on the side of the hill under the bare branches of the chestnut trees, a dozen or so cottages round which hens were silently wandering about. A low shop-window, the lettering almost effaced. Flavières went in. A smell of candles and paraffin. A few picture postcards were turning yellow on a shelf.

'What do you want?' asked an old woman, emerging from the room behind.

'Is there any chance of getting some eggs? Or some meat? I'm an invalid, and you know what it's like in Paris.'

He didn't ask humbly or insinuatingly enough. He was certain she was going to refuse. With an off-hand air, he studied the picture postcards.

'Never mind,' he said, 'I'll try somewhere else. But I'll take this card of the church… Saint-Nicolas, is it?… That rings a bell. Didn't I read about it in the papers way back in 1940—in May, I think. Wasn't there some talk of a suicide?'

'Yes. A woman fell from the church tower.'

'I remember now. Wife of a Paris industrialist, wasn't she?'

'Yes. Madame Gévigne. I shall never forget the name. It was I who found the body. We've had troubles enough since then, but I still think of that poor creature.'

'You wouldn't have any *eau-de-vie*, would you? I don't seem able to keep the cold out.'

She looked at him with eyes that had seen the flux and reflux of war and which no longer expressed anything.

'I dare say I could give you a drop.'

Flavières stuffed the postcard into his pocket and put some coins on the counter. The woman soon came back with a bottle and a glass. It was horrible stuff and burnt his throat.

'A funny idea to throw oneself from a church tower.'

She stowed her hands away under her shawl. Perhaps she didn't think it such a bad idea as all that.

'She made sure of getting what she wanted,' she answered. 'Why, it's sixty feet and more up to that belfry. She fell head first.'

It was on the tip of Flavières' tongue to say:

'I know. I saw her.'

His breath was coming a bit quicker now, but he didn't really think he was suffering. Only, he felt again Madeleine was slipping from him, was really destroying herself for good and all. Each word that fell from the old woman's lips was like a shovelful of earth on the half-filled grave.

'I was all alone in the village at the time,' she went on. 'All the men had been called up, and the women were out working in the fields. At six o'clock I went into the church to say a prayer for my boy who was right up in the front—in the *Corps Franc*, you know.'

She was silent for a minute. A shrunken little woman in black clothes.

'I came out through the sacristy door to take a short cut across the churchyard, so I couldn't help seeing her, lying at the foot of the tower... What a job I had getting through to the *Gendarmerie*...'

She stared at the hens scratching about round the doorway. She was no doubt recalling the fear and oppression of that evening, the gendarmes coming and going and examining the ground by the light of their electric torches.

'It must have been a painful experience,' said Flavières.

'Yes. And to make it worse we had the gendarmes here for a whole week. They would have it the poor woman had been pushed.'

'Pushed? What made them think that?'

'Someone in Sailly said he'd seen a man and a woman in a car, driving this way.'

Flavières lit a cigarette. So that's what it was! Someone had seen him, and he'd been taken for the husband. So he was more than ever responsible for Gévigne's death.

But what was the good of trying to straighten things out now? No one would be interested. He emptied his glass and looked round for something else he could buy. There was nothing but brooms, bundles of firewood, and balls of string.

'Thanks for the *eau-de-vie*,' he murmured.

'You're welcome.'

He went out; he threw away his cigarette, which was making him cough. Back at the church, he hesitated. Should he go in once again, to kneel where she had prayed? No. Her prayer had been in vain. Her body had been blasted into space. He thought of the doctrine of the resurrection of the body. How could Madeleine's body be pieced together again on the Day of Judgment from the atoms into which it had disintegrated?

'*Adieu, Madeleine*,' he whispered, looking up at the cross round which the rooks were cawing.

'Back to Paris, Monsieur?'

'Back to Paris.'

And as the taxi jostled once again along the lane and he turned to cast a final glance at the receding church, he felt sure that at last he was leaving the past behind. At the turning they were just coming to, it would, with that ominous tower,

117

be blotted out for ever. He shut his eyes and dozed all the way back to Paris.

Yet that afternoon he couldn't resist going to see Dr. Ballard and pouring out the whole story, as to a father confessor. With a few omissions, of course. He didn't pronounce the name of Gévigne, nor did he mention the suspicions of the police. He could no longer bottle it up. More than once he almost wept.

'So it comes to this,' said the psychiatrist, 'you're still looking for her. You refuse to believe she's dead.'

Flavières demurred.

'It's not exactly that. She's dead, obviously. I know she is. But I can't help thinking all the same... of course you'll say this is crazy... I can't help thinking of her great-grandmother, Pauline Lagerlac... There was something closer than mere family relationship between them, something...'

'What you're trying to tell me is that this young woman, Madeleine, had already been dead once. That's it, isn't it? That's what you believe?'

'It's not a belief, Doctor. What I've been telling you is what I heard with my own ears and saw with my own eyes.'

'Whatever you heard or saw, it boils down to this: that Madeleine may quite well be alive, since she has come back from the grave once already.'

'If you put it in that way...'

'You don't put it quite so baldly, of course. On the contrary you unconsciously do all you can to blur the outlines... Lie down on the couch, will you?'

The doctor spent a long time testing his reflexes. He made a face.

'Did you drink before?'

'No. I began in Dakar, and little by little…'

'Drugs?'

'Never.'

'I'm wondering whether you really want to be cured.'

'I certainly do.'

'Then you must stop drinking. You must get this woman out of your mind. You must tell yourself she's dead. Permanently dead. Do you understand? Permanently… But once again: do you really want to be cured? Sincerely?'

'Yes, sincerely.'

'Then you must take the bull by the horns. No wobbling. I'll give you a note for a friend of mine who has a home near Nice.'

'You're not going to shut me up?'

'No, no. You're not as bad as that. I'm sending you there partly because of the climate. Coming back from the tropics, you need plenty of sunshine. Have you got any money?'

'Yes.'

'I warn you, it may take quite a long time.'

'I'll stay as long as necessary.'

'Splendid.'

Flavières sat down, feeling weak in the legs. He hardly listened any more to the doctor. He was too busy repeating to himself:

'I want to be cured. Sincerely.'

And to begin the treatment he really regretted having ever loved Madeleine. He was going to start life afresh, turn over a new leaf. Later on, he would be able to approach other women, be like other men… The doctor was still giving him advice. Flavières accepted it, promising this, promising that. Yes, he would take a train south that very evening. Yes, he would stop drinking. Yes, he would rest. Yes… yes… yes.

'Shall I call a taxi for you?' asked the doctor's secretary.

'It'll do me good to walk a bit.'

He went to a travel agency. A notice said that all trains were booked up for a week ahead. Flavières took out his wallet and booked a seat for that very night. All he had to do now was to telephone to the Palais de Justice and his bank. When everything was settled, he wandered about this town in which he was now a stranger. His train went at nine. He'd have dinner at his hotel. That left four hours to kill. He went into a cinema without even bothering to see what was showing. All he wanted was to forget his visit to Dr. Ballard and all those questions he'd been asked. He had never for a moment seriously considered the possibility he might be going mad. Now he was afraid. He felt clammy between the shoulders. He was dying for a drink. Once again he began to hate himself with a shudder of disgust.

The screen lit up and with a blare of music the news was announced. It began with General de Gaulle's visit to Marseilles. Uniforms, flags, bayonets, the crowd being with difficulty pressed back on to the pavement. Close-ups of spectators caught with their mouths wide open, yelling cheers that couldn't be heard. A fat man waving his hat. A woman who turned slowly round and faced the camera. The eyes were pale, and the delicate features recalled some portrait by Lawrence. The camera moved on, but Flavières had had time to recognize her. Half rising from his seat he thrust a terrified face towards the screen.

'Sit down,' cried a voice. 'Sit down.'

He dragged at his collar, his chest bursting with a suffocating cry. He gazed blindly at the marching troops and heard a flourish of trumpets. A rough hand dragged him back into his seat.

TWO

No. It was not Madeleine... He had stayed till the news came round again, and forced himself to look coolly at the picture. He had waited for that face with all his attention concentrated, determined not merely to see it clearly, but to memorize it. And suddenly there it was, for a second or two, and one part of him, as before, had been completely bowled over, while the other part hadn't so much as winced. The woman on the screen was about thirty and inclined to be plump. What else?... Her mouth certainly wasn't the same. Yet the resemblance was undeniable—particularly the eyes. Mobilizing all his faculties, Flavières tried to compare the two faces, but in the end he could only see splodges of colour, as if he had been gazing too long at a bright light.

He went back again in the evening. Never mind: he would take the train tomorrow night... And in the evening he made a discovery: the man next to her was obviously with her—a husband or a lover. He was holding her arm, afraid perhaps of losing her in the crush. On this occasion, Flavières noticed quite a lot he hadn't seen before. The man was well dressed, with a rather showy pearl tie-pin. The woman had a fur coat on.

Flavières came away after the news. The streets were poorly lit. It was still drizzling and he pulled his hat down over his eyes, because of the wind. As he did so, other things came back to him. The man at Marseilles had an overcoat on, but was bareheaded, and behind him, rather out of focus, was the façade of a hotel with three big letters one above the other: RIA. Probably the name of the hotel, lit up at night; something like *Astoria*... What else?

Nothing else. At least nothing factual. But it amused Flavières to see how much he could build on what he had seen. It was such a long time since he'd played the detective. They would be staying in that hotel, and would have dashed out to see the procession pass... As for the resemblance...

There certainly was one. But what of it? A likeness—what a thing to make a fuss about! As though one wasn't reminded of people every day! And he had allowed himself to get upset once again. There was a certain happy man in Marseilles who had a girl whose eyes happened to... As for happy men, they'd be common as dirt now, with a war just over. He'd have to get used to that idea, even if it was a slightly painful one... At his hotel, Flavières made straight for the bar. Admittedly he'd promised that medico... but he needed a glass or two to get his own back on the happy couple staying at the *Astoria*.

'Whisky, please.'

He had three. It didn't matter now that he was going to take himself in hand seriously. He found whisky more efficacious than brandy. Almost at a blow, it dispelled the regrets, the suspicions, the resentments. There always remained something—a confused feeling of enormous injustice—but no alcohol on earth would ever quite remove that. Flavières went to bed. He'd been a fool to postpone his departure.

The next morning, slipping some notes into the ticket collector's hand, he settled down in a first-class compartment. This infinite power of money! But it had come too late. It

122

didn't bring serenity, didn't stop him being feverish, gloomy, or washed out. If he'd been rich before the war, if he'd been able to offer Madeleine... There he was again! He was going to put an end to that.

All the same he hadn't yet thrown away her lighter. Perhaps because of that absurd news-reel. He could do it at any moment, now even—just throw it out of the window. Perhaps he would. There were objects that had evil emanations, slowly poisoning the lives of their owners. Diamonds, for instance. Why not a lighter? Then why not get rid of it? All the same, he knew he never would. It was the one proof that he had once almost been happy. He'd have it put in his coffin.

To be put under the ground hugging a gold lighter! Another absurd idea! Yet he nursed it, and, to the steady rhythm of the wheels, he let his fancy roam... Why had he always been haunted by those underground caverns, by the drip of water in dim light, by the musty air of tunnels, the tortuous entrails of the earth which led down to black pools full of sleeping precious stones? That was where the story had begun, at Saumur, perhaps because of his lonely childhood, which had driven him to books. His favourite, an old mythology, which he had read and re-read, shivering with the chill of death, had been a school prize of his grandfather's. On the fly-leaf was a device and the motto *Labor Omnia Vincit Improbus*, and amongst the mould-marked pages were weird pictures: Sisyphus and his great block of marble, the Danaides pouring water into a sieve, Orpheus emerging from a tomb holding Eurydice by the hand.

His head jolting against the grubby white antimacassar, Flavières watched the real world flit by, hardly seeing it. He felt better: he was playing a game with himself, enjoying his fatigue and his new-found liberty. At Nice he might buy himself a nice little house just outside the town. He'd sleep most of the day. Then when the bats fluttered noiselessly in the evening air, he'd stroll down to the sea-front without thinking of anything. Ah! Not to think! He was advancing towards the black abysses of unconsciousness like the wanderer who quickens his step nearing home.

When the express stopped at Marseilles, Flavières got out. No question of staying there, of course. To make sure of it, he consulted a ticket collector, but the man's answer was unhelpful.

'Your ticket allows you to break your journey for a week.'

All right, if that's how the land lay, he'd stay. Might just as well be frank about it. Nothing to be gained by cheating. But only for a night. Just long enough to check up. He hailed a taxi.

'The *Astoria*.'

'The *Waldorf Astoria*?'

'Naturally,' answered Flavières, chuckling inwardly.

In the hall of the huge hotel, he looked round warily. He knew very well he was playing a game with himself. He was frightening himself—not such a bad game, either. He got a kick out of this uneasiness, this expectation of he knew not what.

'For one night? Or are you staying several days?'

'I don't know… that is… I might be staying.'

'We've only got a suite on the first floor—a large room with a small *salon*.'

'That'll do me nicely.'

In fact he was delighted. He needed this luxury: it was the proper setting for the comedy he was playing. He questioned the lift-boy as he went up.

'When was it General de Gaulle came here?'

'A week ago last Sunday.'

Flavières calculated. Twelve days. That was a long time.

'Have you by any chance noticed a middle-aged man who wears a pearl tie-pin?'

In painful suspense, he waited for the answer, well though he knew it would lead to nothing.

'No… I can't say I have… We get so many here.'

Of course they did. It was nothing to be disappointed about. The first thing he did in his room was to lock the door. An ingrained habit. He had always been a bit mad about locks and bolts and patent security devices, and it was growing on him all the time. He shaved and changed and had a good look at himself in the glass. That was all part of the game. And the eyes he saw in the glass glittered like an actor's. He sauntered down to the bar casually, one hand in a pocket, exactly as if he was expecting to meet an old friend of former days. His eyes glanced round rapidly, pausing for a second at every woman's face. He perched himself on a stool at the bar.

'A whisky.'

Round a narrow space kept clear for dancing, people in deep easy chairs were chatting. Standing near the bar with cigarettes between their fingers, a group of men were talking confidentially. The little flags stuck in glasses, the high-lights on the bottles, the slowly throbbing syncopated music, conspired to make life like a story. It was all slightly feverish, and as Flavières rapidly gulped down his whisky, the fever caught hold of him. He felt ready. For what?

'I'll have another.'

Ready to meet them without flinching. Ready to take one good look at them. That was all. He asked no more… Perhaps they were in the dining-room. He went into the vast room where a waiter promptly adopted him, piloting him towards a table.

'Is Monsieur alone?'

'Yes,' answered Flavières, his mind elsewhere.

A bit dazzled by the lights and intimidated by the people, he sat down without having dared scrutinize the faces. He ordered his meal almost at random, then somewhat awkwardly began looking about him. Lots of officers; few women. Nobody took any notice of him. Why should they? He was of no interest to anybody, and he felt suddenly forced to admit that he was wasting his time. He had been building hopes on an off-chance: there was no reason on earth why the couple he'd seen at the cinema should have been staying at this hotel. They could have put up at any other. Was he going to search the whole town? They could have been merely driving through Marseilles on their way to some other place altogether. And if he did find them, would that get him any further? To find a woman vaguely resembling Madeleine? To kindle once again the fires he'd sworn to let die out?

He forced himself to eat, feeling horribly alone. Why had he made himself go back to Paris, plunging into the tumult of joy and hate that was sweeping over Europe? A pilgrimage? No, that had been merely a pretext. And now he felt like a bit of wreckage washed up on the beach. The only thing for him to do was to go back to Dakar and his dreary occupations. If he needed treatment, there were clinics there.

'Coffee? Liqueurs?'

'Just a *mirabelle*.'

The hands of the clock moved slowly forward. He smoked a cigarette, then another, his eyes dull, his forehead clammy.

People got up and went, amid a clutter of plates and cutlery. No need to stay a week. Tomorrow he would go on to Nice to get a little rest before saying goodbye to France. He too got up, his limbs aching, as though from a long, long journey. He was one of the last to go. On all sides, mirrors reflected the weedy figure slinking between the tables. He went upstairs as slowly as possible, to give himself a last chance, but only met two Americans running down, two steps at a time. In his room at last, he threw his clothes down in a heap and got into bed. He took a long time to go to sleep, and, even when he did, he still seemed to be looking for someone who kept dodging round the corner.

In the morning he woke up with a taste like blood in his mouth and feeling wretched. He dressed in a state of complete discouragement. This was what he had come to, and it was his own fault! If he had forgotten that woman in 1940, if he hadn't deliberately kept himself in a state of mourning, if he'd taken a little more care of his health... Now, in all probability he was a condemned man. How he hated his own twisted, tortuous character, which made him, with a sort of aesthetic dilettantism, dally with dubious emotions! He gently massaged his eyelids and pressed his forehead—a gesture that was destined to become a habit... A sick man, was he?... Well, anyhow, people would have to speak kindly to him in future.

He finished dressing, in a hurry to look at the time-table. Marseilles seemed to him a forbidding place with its smoke, its noise and bustle. He was in a hurry, too, to be coddled by motherly women in white aprons, to bask in silence. He was busy constructing another romance to ward off the terrible idea which nevertheless kept forcing its way into his consciousness: *'I'm done for.'*

His head was still aching as he walked along the thickly carpeted corridor. Breathing became a little easier as he went slowly downstairs to the reception desk. In a small room opening on the right, people were having their coffee and rolls, robust people whose jaws moved with repulsive gusto. Flavières saw a stout man... was he dreaming?... in whose tie...

Mon Dieu! Could that be him?... A well-dressed man of fifty, who was cutting a roll in two as he chatted with a young woman, whose back was turned to Flavières. She had very long, dark hair, partly concealed by the collar of the fur coat thrown over her shoulders. To look at her face he would have to go into the room... He would. Presently, though. For the moment he was too upset. These silly emotional shocks weren't good for him at all. Mechanically he fished a cigarette out of his case, then hastily replaced it. He mustn't start smoking before breakfast. He tried to convince himself that he wasn't remotely interested in the couple at the table, then, giving up the pretence, he asked at the desk in a low voice:

'That man there... the one going bald, talking to the woman in a fur coat... do you know his name?'

'Almaryan.'

'Almaryan!... What's he do?'

The man at the desk winked.

'A bit of everything... There's plenty of money to be made these days if you know the ropes. He does.'

'Is that his wife?'

'Oh no. He never keeps the same one long.'

'Can I see the time-table?'

'Certainly, Monsieur.'

Flavières sat in the hall turning its pages, but he couldn't keep his eyes on it for long. The woman had turned a little and from where he was sitting he could get a fairly good view of her. A sudden certitude blazed up within him. Madeleine! How could he have hesitated? She had changed, of course. She was a little fatter in the face, and older. It was another Madeleine and yet the same Madeleine... The same!

He sank gently back in his chair, leaning his head against the back. He hadn't the strength to take out his handkerchief to wipe the perspiration from his face. He felt he would lose consciousness altogether if he moved a muscle or even if he framed a thought. So he sat absolutely still. His eyes were closed but the lids couldn't shut out the image of Madeleine which burnt into his brain.

'If it's her, I'll die,' he muttered, letting the time-table slip from his hands on to the floor.

Slowly and cautiously he pulled himself together. He really mustn't lose his head because he'd caught sight of Madeleine's double. He opened his eyes. No, she wasn't a double. What is it that gives absolute certitude to the act of recognition? He knew that Madeleine was sitting there, opposite the portly Almaryan, in the same way as he knew that he wasn't dreaming, that he was really and truly Flavières, that he was suffering agonies. He suffered because, at the same time, he was equally certain Madeleine was dead.

Almaryan stood up and took the young woman by the arm. Flavières quickly picked up the time-table and buried himself in it while they passed. He saw the bottom of the fur coat and elegant shoes. When he finally looked up, he saw them through the gate of the lift, the shadows of which on her face had somewhat the same effect as that little veil she had worn, and he felt again a sharp stab of his old love. He got up irresolutely, wondering whether she had seen him. He returned the time-table to the desk.

'Will you be keeping your room, Monsieur?'

'Of course!'

All the morning he sauntered about in the sunshine, exploring the old port, whose activity was divided between civilian trade and war shipments. The stones trembled as military convoys rumbled away. Shivering, Flavières immersed himself in the clatter and the hubbub, jostling with the crowd. There would never be people enough in the world to stave off his fear. For he had seen the body. So had Gévigne. So had the old woman who had laid Madeleine out. The police had investigated her suicide, even if none too intelligently. There must have been at least ten people to verify her death... In that case the woman with Almaryan wasn't Madeleine... He drank a *pastis* in a bar on the Canebière. He would restrict himself to that. Already he could feel the faint delirium kindle within him. He lit a cigarette with the lighter, that lighter which couldn't lie, which was there in his hand, polished by his fingers which had fondled it so often in silent prayer, as though it had been a bead in a rosary... Madeleine had died at the foot of that church tower... And, before her, Pauline... Nevertheless...

He had to have a whisky, because the idea that had flashed into his mind was so extraordinary that he needed all his faculties to examine it properly. He could remember every word of their conversation at the Louvre.

'I've already walked through these rooms on the arm of a man,' she had said. 'He was like you, only he had sidewhiskers.'

How clear it became all of a sudden. At the time he had been unable to understand; he had been too full of life, too blinded by prejudices, he hadn't yet been initiated by suffering and illness... Now he was quite able to accept the truth, as consoling as it had so far been inconceivable. Just as Pauline's spirit had housed itself in Madeleine's body, so Madeleine's had now... It could even be the same with himself. Perhaps in some far-off forgotten time he had already gazed at that purplish sea, those brown sails... He, too, might have been dead before—more than once perhaps, many times... If only one could be sure! But Madeleine had been.

If he was right, why should he be afraid? What was there to be afraid of? Of waking up? Of no longer believing the miracle? Of having chased foolishly a will-o'-the-wisp? No. He was only afraid of seeing her again, as he would have to speak to her. Nothing would hold him back. And of course he wanted to. Yet would he be able to bear the look in her eyes, the sound of her voice?

That evening, he changed for dinner. He put on a black suit. To convince himself he was still in mourning. The moment he went into the bar, he saw her in the dining-room. With her chin resting on her hands, she seemed to be dreaming, while Almaryan talked in a low voice to the head-waiter, presumably trying to dodge the food restrictions. Flavières sat down, making a sign to the barman, who, knowing him by now, promptly poured out a whisky. Two or three couples were dancing. Through the wide-open folding doors to the dining-room, he could inspect the diners and watch the trolleys laden with *hors-d'oeuvres* being slowly wheeled along by white-clad waiters. She looked sad, and it was her sadness which fascinated

Flavières. Already in the old days... Though Gévigne must have given her everything she wanted. It was strange to think that others had inherited her fortune, while she was poor, obliged to cling to a man like this Almaryan, who looked like a wily caliph. Her ear-rings were in bad taste and her nails were painted. How much more distinguished the other Madeleine had been! Flavières had the impression he was looking at a badly dubbed film, with some nonentity speaking the part of a star. She ate little, now and again taking a sip of wine. She looked relieved when at last Almaryan got up. They came into the bar and found themselves a table. Flavières swivelled round on his stool, but he could hear Almaryan behind him ordering the coffee. Was this the moment? Would he ever have the courage?

He handed the barman a note and slipped off his stool. He had only to turn round and take three steps forward. Then four years of misery would be lifted from his heart; past and present would be reconciled; Madeleine would be there before him, just as if they had left each other the previous evening after a trip to Versailles. Perhaps she would even forget how she had slipped away from him...

And suddenly he did it. He turned; he took the three steps forward; he bent ceremoniously over the young woman, and asked her to dance with him. For a few seconds he had a close view of Almaryan's slightly yellowing cheeks and his velvety black eyes. Then he saw Madeleine's face raised towards him, her pale blue eyes which expressed nothing but annoyance. She accepted sulkily. Was it possible she simply hadn't recognized him? As they swayed to and fro over the dancing floor, Flavières' throat was strangled. He felt as though he were breaking all the ten commandments at a go, flouting some inexorable taboo.

'My name's Flavières,' he murmured at last. 'Doesn't that ring a bell?'

Politely, she seemed making an effort to recall it.

'No. I'm sorry... I really can't say that it does.'

'And what's your name?' he asked.

'Renée Sourange.'

He was on the point of contradicting her when it occurred to him that she had necessarily acquired a new name, and he was more disturbed than ever. He studied her sidelong. The forehead, the colour of the eyes, the line of the nose, the prominent cheek-bones—each one of those details was just as he had known it of old, just as he had cherished it in the secret recesses of his memory. If he had shut his eyes, he could have imagined himself once again in the Louvre... But there were other things: the way the new Madeleine did her hair lacked style, her mouth had lost its line, despite the efforts of lipstick. Not that it mattered: she was almost better as she was, because less intimidating. He could approach her more easily now, feeling her to be made of the same clay as he was. He had been afraid of embracing a shadow. He found her a woman, and he reproached himself for desiring her already, as though he was profaning something very profound and very pure.

'You used to live in Paris before the occupation, I believe?'

'No. In London.'

'Come on! Didn't you go in for painting?'

'No. I have done a little to while away the time, that's all.'

'Did you ever go to Rome?'

'Never.'

'Why are you trying to deceive me?'

She looked at him with those pale, slightly vacant eyes that were unforgettable.

'I'm not doing anything of the kind, I assure you.'

'This morning you saw me in the hall. You recognized me. And now you're pretending…'

She tried to break away from him, but Flavières held her tightly against him, blessing the music which showed no signs of stopping.

'Excuse me,' he said.

After all, for years and years Madeleine hadn't known she was Pauline Lagerlac. It wasn't astonishing if Renée didn't yet know she was Madeleine.

'I'm completely drunk,' he said to himself.

And out loud, with a jerk of his head towards Almaryan:

'Is he jealous?'

'Far from it,' she answered sadly.

'Black market, I suppose?'

'Of course. Are you in it too?'

'No. I'm a lawyer… Is he very busy?'

'Yes. He's out a lot.'

'Then I could see you sometimes during the day?'

She didn't answer. He allowed his hand to slip down to her waist.

'If you need me,' he murmured, 'I'm in Room 17. You won't forget?'

'No… I must go back to him now.'

Almaryan was smoking a cigar as he read the *Dauphiné Libéré*.

'I think he gets along very well without you,' said Flavières. 'Till tomorrow, then.'

He bowed, then went upstairs, forgetting he hadn't had any dinner. In the lift, he asked:

'Monsieur Almaryan—what's the number of his room?'

'He's got a suite. No. 11.'

'What's the name of the woman he's got with him?'

'Renée Sourange.'

'That her real name?'

'No reason why it shouldn't be! It's what's on her *carte d'identité*.'

Contrary to his usual habit—he was inclined to be close-fisted—he gave a handsome tip. He would have given a lot more to know… Ah! If only he could *know*! He drank three glasses of water before going to bed, but without succeeding in dissipating the fog in which he was engulfed. He was frightened again: he had to admit it. Surely she must have recognized him! Unless… Drunk though he might be, the three alternatives stood out clearly: either she was pretending, or she was suffering from amnesia, or she wasn't Madeleine.

He woke up in a fury. As he saw things now, it was obviously high time for him to get into the hands of that doctor at Nice. He blushed to think of his theories of the previous day. He had nothing further to do in Marseilles. Health must come first, and this girl who looked like Madeleine could go to the devil.

All the same, he watched for Almaryan's departure, and promptly looked for No. 11. He knocked lightly several times, as though he was a familiar visitor.

'Who's that?'

'Flavières.'

She opened the door. Her eyes were red, her eyelids swollen. She hadn't dressed.

'Well, Renée, what's the matter now?'

She began crying again. He shut the door and bolted it.

'What's the matter, my little one? Tell me all about it.'

'He's had enough of me. He's turfing me out.'

Flavières studied her without indulgence. It was Madeleine, certainly, a Madeleine who had been disloyal to him—with Almaryan, with others perhaps. He clenched his fists in his trouser-pockets. His smile was a little twisted.

'What a fuss about nothing!' he said with forced jocularity. 'What do you want him for? Aren't I here to fill the gap?'

Renée's tears flowed faster than ever.

'No,' she cried. 'No... Not you!'

'Why not?' he asked, bending over her.

THREE

> *Monsieur le Directeur,*
>
> *I have the honour to inform you that the sum indicated has been paid into your account at Marseilles. Though this withdrawal cannot be said seriously to embarrass the firm, I am bound to point out the irregularity of the proceeding, a repetition of which might well have more serious consequences. I trust your health is no longer causing you anxiety and that we may shortly be seeing you in Paris again. All goes well here, and business is satisfactory.*

The signature, after the assurance of the writer's devoted sentiments, etc., was J. Traboul.

Flavières tore the letter up in a rage. He easily lost his temper. Particularly now.

'Bad news?' asked Renée.

'No. Not really. Just another little bit of Traboul's nonsense.'

'Who's Traboul?'

'My junior partner. To listen to him, you'd think the world was coming to an end tomorrow. He's always like that. And Dr. Ballard told me I needed rest... Rest!'

He paced angrily up and down for a moment, then said roughly:

'Come on. We'll go out for a breath of fresh air.'

He regretted his luxurious suite in the *Waldorf Astoria*. Here in the *Hôtel de France* the rooms were small and forbidding, and horribly expensive into the bargain. The only advantage of the place was that they didn't risk running into Almaryan. Flavières took out a cigarette and struck a match. He didn't dare use the lighter now... She was sitting at the dressing-table, doing her hair.

'I don't like it like that,' he grunted. 'Can't you do it differently?'

'How?'

'I don't know how. In a bun at the back of your neck, perhaps.'

He had said that on the impulse of the moment. And was already cursing himself for doing so. What was the good of provoking the same old quarrel which had been going on for days, with its exhausting scenes and deceptive reconciliations? They turned round each other like animals in a cage, growling and showing their claws, except when they slept to dream of the wide open spaces.

'I'll wait for you downstairs.'

He made straight for the bar and scowled at the smiling barman. Men were all alike behind their counters, falsely ingratiating, silkily whispering their wares as though to allay suspicion. Flavières ordered a drink. There was no longer any reason why he shouldn't drink—now that he was sure! It was all very well for her to swear she wasn't Madeleine: he knew she was. He knew it with an absolute certainty, a certainty not merely of the brain but of all his flesh and blood. As if she had been, not his mistress, but his child. And, as a matter of fact, she was so little his mistress. He could do without that side of her so easily. He was even a little shocked that Madeleine could lend herself to carnal pleasures. What he loved in her—and it had been so all along—was... it was difficult to explain...

was that she wasn't quite real. And now, on the contrary, she seemed anxious to prove that she was just like any other woman, that she was Renée in fact, a person without either mystery or grace. And yet… If only she would consent to yield up her secret, how wonderful it would be! He would be delivered from his solitude. For, in the last resort, it was he who belonged to the dead, she to the living!

She came downstairs. He saw her coming, her mouth twisted by a vague grimace. He didn't like the colour of her dress. Not only the colour: it was badly cut and rather showy. She needed higher heels too… and then… well, the whole of her face needed to be slightly remodelled, the cheeks hollowed out a little to make the most of those touchingly prominent cheek-bones, the eyebrows faintly pencilled to restore to them the touch of bewilderment of someone who had strayed into an alien world. Only the eyes were perfect, only they were the absolute proof. Flavières paid for his drink and went to meet her. He would have liked to throw his arms round her, to embrace her; yes, perhaps to suffocate her.

'I was as quick as I could be,' she said.

He almost shrugged his shoulders. She no longer knew how to find the right words. Even her way of slipping her hand under his arm jarred on him. She was too timid, too submissive. She was slightly afraid of him. Nothing could be more irritating than that. They walked in silence side by side. He was thinking:

'If I'd been promised this a month ago, I'd have died of joy.'

Now that it had happened, he had never been so miserable.

In front of the shop-windows she hung back a little. That annoyed him too.

'You had to go without a lot of things during the war, I suppose?'

'Everything.'

The accent of poverty touched him.

'Then Almaryan rigged you out, I suppose?'

He knew very well the words would wound her, yet he couldn't hold them back. By her grip on his arm, he knew she winced.

'I was lucky to find him.'

Now it was his turn to be wounded. So it went on. That was the game. But he couldn't chuck it up.

'Look here…' he began angrily.

But what was the good? He dragged her towards the centre of the town.

'No need to go so fast,' she complained. 'As we're only out for a walk.'

He didn't answer. It was he who was now looking in the shop-windows. Presently he found what he was looking for.

'Come on. You can ask questions later.'

A shop-walker bowed, his hands clasped.

'Dresses,' said Flavières curtly.

'First floor. The lift's over there.'

He had made up his mind. And Traboul would jolly well have to stump up. A sharp pleasure tingled within him. She would confess! She would be forced to!… The lift-boy shut the gate and they went up.

'*Chéri*,' whispered Renée.

'Be quiet.'

He went up to one of the shop-assistants.

'Show us some dresses. The most elegant ones you have.'

'Certainly, Monsieur.'

Flavières sat down. He was a little out of breath, almost as if he'd been running. The girl produced several dresses, watching for Renée's response, but it was he who chipped in:

'That one.'

'The black one?'

'Yes. The black one.'

And to Renée:

'Will you try it on?… To please me.'

She hesitated, blushing under the eyes of the girl, who was trying to size them up. Then she went meekly into the cubicle. Flavières got up and began pacing up and down. It was like old times: he was waiting for her. With the same throbbing anxiety, the same sense of suffocation. He was once again alive. At the bottom of his pocket he gripped the lighter fiercely. Then, as the time didn't pass quickly enough, as the suspense became unbearable, he looked for a grey suit from a row hanging on a rod. It had to be grey. There were several, but none quite the right grey. No grey, of course, would ever be exactly like the one he remembered. Was that because he had idealized it for so long? Could he be sure his memory wasn't playing him false?

The door of the cubicle opened. He swung round and received the same shock as at the *Waldorf*. There she was: Madeleine come to life again. Yes, it was Madeleine who stopped suddenly as though recognizing him, Madeleine who came towards him, rather pale and with the same wistful, enquiring look he knew so well. He held out his thin hand, but immediately dropped it again. No. Something was still wrong. How was it he hadn't at once noticed those ear-rings which spoilt everything?

'Take them off,' he growled in an undertone.

As she didn't understand, he took the arrogant things off with his own hands—a little too roughly. Then, stepping back, he examined her again with that despair of the painter who can't get the exact effect he's striving after.

'Good,' he said. 'Madame will keep that dress on… And we'll take this grey suit too, if it's the same size… Is it?… Well, do it up, please… and tell us where the shoe department is.'

Renée offered no resistance. Perhaps she understood why Flavières studied each pair of shoes with such a critical eye, rejecting one for this reason, another for that. He chose some neat shiny ones.

'Now. Let's see you walk in them.'

Perched up on high heels in the close-fitting black dress she looked another person, almost ethereal.

'That'll do,' he snapped.

The girl who was serving them looked up in surprise and he quickly changed his tone to say:

'They'll do perfectly. Wrap the others up.'

He took Renée by the hand and dragged her over to a mirror.

'Now look,' he murmured. 'Look at yourself… Madeleine!'

'Please…' she begged.

'Come on! Just one more effort… That woman in black you're looking at… that's not Renée Sourange… Try to remember.'

She was visibly suffering. Fear distorted her face, and the other face, the real one, was only visible in an occasional intangible reflection.

He hadn't finished. He dragged Madeleine to the lift. He'd see about the hair later. For the moment it was the scent that mattered. That would call up the past more than anything. Yes. He was going to see this through, regardless of the consequences.

They hadn't got the scent he wanted. In vain he tried to describe it.

'No,' said the girl in the perfumery department, 'I'm afraid I don't quite see…'

'I'm sure you've got it… How can I describe it? It smells something like freshly dug earth, like withered flowers.'

'Unless you mean Chanel No. 3.'

'Perhaps.'

'It's not being made any more. You might find a bottle in a little shop that had some old stock. I'm afraid we can't help you.'

Renée tugged at his sleeve but he lingered there, thoughtfully fingering the bottles. Without that perfume the resurrection would be incomplete. Finally he allowed her to lead him away, but he didn't leave the store till he'd bought her a little hat of very soft felt and subtle line. While he was paying, he looked out of the corner of his eye at the startlingly new yet familiar silhouette at his side, and a glint of indulgence warmed his heart. It was he who took Renée's arm. No, Madeleine's!

'Why are you doing all these silly things?' she asked.

'Why?… Because I want you to discover yourself. Because I want to know the truth.'

She bridled. He could feel her aloofness, her hostility, but he held her tightly against him. She wasn't going to get away again. She'd give in in the end.

'I want you to be perfect,' he went on. 'Almaryan is wiped off the slate. He has never existed.'

They walked on in silence for a minute or two, but, try as he might, he was unable to leave the subject alone.

'You can't be Renée Sourange,' he said. 'No. You must listen to me. You can see I'm not angry; I'm speaking quite calmly.'

She heaved a sigh. That always maddened him, but he just managed to keep his temper.

'Yes, I know… You're Renée; you lived in London with your Uncle Charles, your father's brother; you were born at Dambremont in the Vosges, a tiny village on the river… You've told me all that over and over again. But it's not true. It can't be true. You're making a mistake.'

'For heaven's sake don't let's start that all over again.'

'I'm not going over it again. All I want is that you try to remember. If you probe a little, you'll find there's a hitch somewhere. Perhaps you were ill at some time or other, seriously ill.'

'I assure you…'

'There are illnesses which do queer things to people.'

'I couldn't forget an illness. All I've ever had was scarlet fever at the age of ten.'

'No. It can't be all.'

'I'm fed up with this.'

He was determined to be patient, as though Madeleine was an invalid, an extremely fragile person who mustn't be jolted, yet her obstinacy infuriated him.

'You've told me hardly anything about your childhood,' he said. 'I want to know all about it.'

And, as they were passing the Musée Grobet-Labadié, he added:

'Let's go in here. It's a good place for a talk.'

But he was no sooner in the entrance hall than he knew it was a mistake: his inner torment would start again more cruelly than ever. Indeed, the sound of their steps, the silence of the things round them, the paintings and portraits, reminded him of the Louvre with aching intensity. And, as she lowered her voice so as not to disturb the sanctity of the empty rooms, she suddenly reacquired Madeleine's tone, the veiled contralto that gave such value to her confidences.

Flavières listened less to her words than to their strange music. She told him about her childhood. Inevitably it was similar to Madeleine's. Like Madeleine she was an only child… And, dressed as she now was, he longed to take her into his arms. Stopping in front of a picture of the Vieux Port, he asked in a shaky voice:

'Do you like that sort of painting?'

'No. I don't know. I'm quite ignorant of painting, you know.'

He sighed and took her on into a room full of models of boats and ships—caravels, galleys, tartans, and a three-decker complete with all its guns and an exquisite network of rigging.

'Tell me some more.'

'What do you want to know?'

'Everything. What you did. What you thought about.'

'Oh, I was a little girl much like any other, I suppose. Perhaps not so light-hearted as some… I read a lot. I liked old tales and legends.'

'You too!'

'Don't all children?… I used to wander about on the hills. I told myself stories. I saw life as a fairy-tale… I was wrong!'

They went into the collection of Roman Antiquities. Statues and busts with blind staring eyes and short curly hair stood peacefully dreaming against the walls. Flavières' uneasiness increased. Some of those consuls reminded him of Gévigne, even recalling snatches of his conversation.

'I want you to keep an eye on my wife… I'm worried about her…'

They were both dead, but their voices lived on. So did their physical shapes… And Madeleine, as in the old days, was walking by his side.

'You never lived in Paris?' he asked.

'No. I went through once, on my way to England. That's all.'

'I'm questioning her like a suspect,' he thought, 'as though she'd committed a crime.'

With that reflection he lost the thread, couldn't remember what he'd been leading up to. He was bitter and disappointed. He listened to Madeleine absent-mindedly. Was she lying? What reason would she have to lie? And how could she glibly invent all the details she was now giving him? The most sceptical couldn't fail to be convinced she was none other than Renée Sourange.

'You're not listening,' she said. 'Is anything the matter?'

'No… I'm just a bit tired. It's stuffy in here.'

They walked rapidly through several rooms to the exit. Flavières was glad to see the sun again and hear again the roar of the traffic. He wanted to be alone. He needed a drink.

'I'll leave you here. I've got to go to the Food Office to see about my supplementary rations. Amuse yourself. Buy yourself what you like. Here!'

He shoved a bundle of notes into her hand, then promptly regretted the impulse. Why had he made her his mistress? That had spoilt everything. He had turned her into a sort of freak who was neither Madeleine nor Renée.

'Don't be too long,' she called after him.

When she was twenty or thirty yards away he nearly ran back

146

to her. Her gait, the slight movement of her shoulders—every detail as she walked away along the sunny pavement was exactly as it had always been. Now she was going to cross the road. *Mon Dieu!* He was going to lose her, and it was he who had opened his arms to let her go.

No—idiot that he was! She wasn't going to run away... No danger of that! She wasn't such a fool. She would be waiting for him obediently at their hotel.

He went straight into a café. He was at the end of his tether. 'A *pastis.*'

The cool drink didn't calm him down. Not for a second could he banish the problem from his mind, nor could he get any nearer to a solution. Renée was Madeleine, yet she wasn't *altogether* Madeleine. What sort of a show would your Dr. Ballards put up if they had to find an answer to a riddle like that?... Unless, of course, he, Flavières, had been completely mistaken from the start, his memory having played him a trick. After all, he had only known the old Madeleine for a very short time... And with all that had happened in between... No, that wouldn't wash either. Had not she haunted him day and night? Had not her image been perpetually before his mind's eye, like an icon? He could have recognized Madeleine with his eyes shut, from her presence alone.

The truth was that she was different from other women, belonging to another species. And just as Pauline had been a bit lost in the part of Madeleine, so was the latter in that of Renée. As though her spirit hesitated a little before abandoning itself to a new incarnation... Perhaps in the end she would become Renée completely... No. He would never allow that... Because Renée was an ageing woman, because she had neither Madeleine's distinction nor her charm, because, lastly, she was so obstinately holding out against the proofs he lay before her.

He ordered another drink. Proofs? Could he honestly call them that? When he couldn't put a single scrap of evidence before her which could be verified! He was *morally* certain. No more than that. To break down Madeleine's resistance, to force her to admit she was hiding behind the identity of Renée, he needed some solid, material fact. But what?

The alcohol began to seep through his veins. Encouraged, he began to see the problem less gloomily. Perhaps, after all, there was a solid fact that wouldn't be too difficult to establish. More than once already, he had seen Renée's identity card, which said: *Sourange, Renée Catherine, née le 24 octobre 1916 à Dambremont, Vosges.*

Pensively, he paid the bill. Yes. His idea was perfectly reasonable. He jumped on to a tram going towards the post office. He tried not to think now, afraid of stumbling on an objection. He studied the commonplace faces of the people standing with him on the rear platform, and he could almost have wished himself one of them, for they were not afraid.

At the post office he queued up patiently for a telephone call. If the lines were working again and not monopolized by priority calls, he would soon know…

'Can I put through a call to Dambremont?'

'What Department?'

'Vosges.'

'Dambremont? Probably have to go through Gérardmer. In that case…'

He turned to another man.

'You ought to know… Dambremont, Vosges… A gentleman wants to telephone.'

The other looked up.

'Dambremont? It's flat. The Boches didn't leave a stone standing… What's it for?'

'An extract from the register of births,' said Flavières.

'There's nothing left at all. Just a heap of rubble.'

'What can I do then?'

The man shrugged his shoulders and went back to his work. Flavières walked away. So there was nothing left. No records. Nothing but that identity card dated November 1944… That didn't prove that Renée had lived at the same time as Madeleine… He went down the steps sadly. It was lacking. No one would ever be able to establish the fact that they had been alive simultaneously, that they were thus really and truly two separate beings. If they weren't…

Flavières walked aimlessly. He oughtn't to have started drinking. He oughtn't to have tried to telephone. His mind had been more tranquil before. Why couldn't he simply love this woman and leave it at that, instead of poisoning their relations by his ceaseless probings… All the same, the fact that he'd drawn a blank at the post office proved nothing. Very well, then—ought he to go to Dambremont and start rummaging in the ruins? There he was again! Incorrigible, odious!… And supposing she got tired of his suspicions, his reproaches, his ill-tempered tyranny, and left? Yes, think of it! Supposing she packed her bags one day and left?

The idea was enough to make his legs feel weak under him. He stopped at the corner of the street, his hand pressed to his side, like an invalid fearing a heart attack. Then he went on again slowly, his shoulders sagging. Poor Madeleine! He seemed to take a delight in making her suffer… But why, why did she refuse to speak?

Suppose she did. Suppose she turned suddenly on him and said:

'Yes. I was dead. I've come back from down there. And these blue eyes of mine have seen…'

Would he not fall dead himself, struck by lightning?

'Now I really am going out of my mind,' he thought. 'But if you carry logic to its uttermost extreme, isn't that the same thing as madness?'

At the hotel he hesitated, then, catching sight of a florist, went and bought some carnations and mimosa. That would brighten up their room. Renée would feel less of a prisoner. He took the lift, and the heady scent of the mimosa in the little cabin reminded him of that other one… His obsession returned treacherously. When he opened the door of his room he was again drooping with disgust and despair. Renée was lying on the bed. Flavières flung the flowers down on the table.

'Well?' he said.

No! She wasn't crying, was she? He rushed forward, his fists clenched.

'What's the matter? Tell me quickly. What's happened?'

He took her head in his hands and turned her face to the light. 'My poor child!'

He had never seen Madeleine cry. But neither had he forgotten her wet face when he had dragged her out of the Seine. He shut his eyes.

'Stop crying,' he murmured. 'Please stop crying. At once. You've no idea what it does to me.'

And, suddenly angry, he stamped his foot.

'Stop, I tell you! Stop!'

She sat up and drew him towards her. For a minute they sat quite still, as though waiting for something. Then Flavières put his arm round her shoulders.

'Forgive me. My nerves are all jangled. Forgive me. You know how I love you.'

The day faded slowly. Below, a tram screeched round a bend. Green flashes from the contact with the overhead wire were reflected in the windows opposite. The mimosa smelt of wet earth. Pressed close to Renée, Flavières calmed down. What was the point of his incessant quest? Wasn't he happy at this woman's side? Of course he would have preferred her to be Madeleine. But it wasn't too difficult in the twilight to imagine she was. Madeleine in her black dress escaped for a moment from the shadows into which she had dissolved.

'It's time we went down to dinner,' she whispered.

'No. Let's stay here. I'm not hungry.'

It was a marvellous respite. She would be his so long as the night lasted, so long as her face was no more than a splash of paleness in the hollow of his shoulder... Madeleine... He sank gently into a serenity such as he had never known. No. They were not two... no need to try and explain it... He was no longer afraid.

'I'm no longer afraid,' he murmured.

She stroked his forehead. He could feel her breath on his cheek. The scent of the mimosa seemed to be swelling, filling the whole room. He gently pushed away this body, whose warmth entered into him, and seized the hand that had been caressing his face.

'Come.'

The bed hollowed on his side. He still held her hand. He handled it delicately as though he would count the fingers. He now recognized the bony wrist, the short thumb, the rounded nails. How could he ever have forgotten?... God! How sleepy he was. He sank into the shadows in which his memories were still leading their strange lives: in front of him the steering wheel of a car and on it a small hand full of nervous energy, the same that had undone the packet tied with blue ribbon and taken out the card. *A Eurydice ressuscitée*... He opened his eyes. Beside him lay a motionless figure. For a moment he listened to her breathing, then, raising himself on one elbow, he bent over the invisible face and let his lips touch the closed eyelids which flickered in an almost imperceptible response.

'Won't you really tell me who you are?'

Tears wetted the warm eyelids and he tasted them pensively. Then he looked for his handkerchief under the pillow. He couldn't find it.

'I'll be back in a second.'

Softly he slipped into the bathroom. Renée's bag was there on the dressing-table among the cosmetics. He opened it and delved into it, but found no handkerchief. On the other hand, his fingers came in contact with something which intrigued him—some oval beads, a necklace. Yes, it was a necklace. He took it to the window and held it up in the pale glaucous light which filtered through the frosted glass. The amber beads glowed faintly golden. His hands began to tremble. There was no room for doubt. It was the necklace of Pauline Lagerlac.

FOUR

'You're drinking too much,' said Renée.

She quickly glanced at the next table, fearing to have spoken too loudly. She knew very well that for some days now people had been looking askance at Flavières.

Defiantly he emptied his glass at a draught. His cheeks were pale except for a little hectic flush over his cheek-bones.

'It isn't this phony burgundy that'll go to my head,' he retorted.

'All the same… You're doing yourself no good.'

'Precisely! I'm doing myself no good. I spend my life doing myself no good. You can't teach me anything on that score.'

He glared at her, without any reason. She studied the menu to avoid those hard, desperate eyes, which watched her unceasingly. The waiter came up.

'A sweet?'

'Just a tartlet,' said Renée.

'The same for me,' said Flavières.

As soon as the waiter had gone, he leant over towards her.

'You don't eat enough… In the old days…'

His lips trembled slightly as he finished the sentence.

'… In the old days you thought nothing of putting down three or four *brioches*.'

'What do you mean?'

'Yes, you did… Think a little… In the Galeries Lafayette…'

'That old story!'

'Yes. The story of the time when I was happy.'

Flavières' breath came quickly. He searched in his pockets, then in Renée's bag for cigarettes and matches, keeping his eyes on her all the time.

'You oughtn't to smoke so much either,' she faltered.

'I know. That's another thing that's doing me no good. But I happen to like being ill. There! And if I peg out…'

He lit his cigarette and waved the match in front of Renée's eyes.

'… If I peg out, that doesn't matter either. You told me so yourself once. You said: "It doesn't hurt to die".'

She shrugged her shoulders, at the end of her patience.

'Yes,' he went on, 'and I can tell you the exact spot where you said it. It was by the Seine, at Courbevoie. You see, I have a memory.'

He laughed. He had his elbows on the table and one eye half shut because of the smoke from his cigarette. The waiter brought the tartlets.

'Go on,' said Flavières. 'Eat them both. I've finished.'

'People are looking at us,' pleaded Renée.

'What? Haven't I even the right to say I've finished eating? If my appetite's satisfied, it's a good advertisement for the house.'

'I don't know what's the matter with you this evening.'

'Nothing, *chérie*. Nothing. I'm in excellent spirits… Why don't you eat them with a spoon? You used to.'

She pushed her plate away, snatched up her bag, and got up.

'Really. You're impossible.'

He got up too. She was quite right: everybody was looking at them, but that didn't disturb him in the least. Other people no longer existed. He was far beyond minding anything that was said about him. Which of them could stand one hour of what he was living through day in, day out?

He caught Renée up at the lift. The lift-boy eyed them surreptitiously. She blew her nose, hid her face behind her bag, pretending to powder her nose. She became truly beautiful like that, on the verge of tears. Moreover it was only right that she should share his martyrdom. They went down the long corridor in silence. Entering their room, she threw her bag down on the bed.

'We can't go on like this,' she said. 'These continual allusions to something I can't understand… this restless life we lead… no… it would be better for us to separate… Otherwise you'll end by driving me out of my mind.'

She wasn't crying, but her eyes glistened with a quivering moisture. Flavières smiled sadly.

'Do you remember the church of Saint-Nicolas?… You had just got up from your knees. You were pale, just as you are now.'

She sank heavily on to the edge of the bed, as though some invisible hand had pressed her down. Her lips hardly moved.

'Saint-Nicolas?'

'Yes, that church tucked away in the depths of the country not far from Mantes… You were on the point of dying.'

'On the point of dying? Me?'

Suddenly she threw herself face downwards on the bed, burying her head in her arms. Sobs shook her shoulders. Flavières knelt down beside her. He wanted to stroke her head, but she shrank away from him.

'Don't touch me,' she cried.

'Are you frightened of me?'

155

'Yes.'

'Do you think I'm drunk?'

'No.'

'Mad, then?'

'Yes.'

He stood up for a moment and was lost in thought. He ran his hand over his forehead.

'That's not impossible… All the same, there's that necklace… No, let me finish… Why don't you wear it?'

'Because I don't like it. I've told you so already.'

'Or was it because you were afraid I might recognize it?… That's it, isn't it?'

'No.'

'Do you swear it?'

'Of course I do.'

He considered that answer, making a complicated pattern on the carpet with his toe.

'And, according to you, it was a present from Almaryan?'

She raised herself on one elbow and tucked her legs up. He looked at her miserably.

'Almaryan told me he'd bought it in Paris. At an antique shop in the Rue du Faubourg Saint-Honoré.'

'How long ago?'

'I've told you that too. Why do you always make me repeat the same thing over and over again?'

'Never mind. Repeat it. How long ago?'

'Six months.'

That was possible, of course… no, it wasn't. Such a coincidence was inconceivable.

'You're lying,' he said.

'What should I want to lie for?'

'Come on. You might just as well confess and have done with it. You're Madeleine Gévigne.'

'No. Don't say that again. You're simply torturing me. If you're still in love with that woman, you'd better leave me... I'd rather you did... I'll clear out. I've had enough of this.'

'That woman... is dead, and...'

He hesitated. He was terribly thirsty, and kept coughing to cover the burning dryness of his throat. Correcting himself, he went on:

'Or rather she was dead for a while... Only, is that possible?'

'No,' she moaned. 'Don't go on, please...'

Again, the pale mask of dread spread over her face. He drew away from her.

'You've nothing to be afraid of. You can see I don't want to hurt you... I know I say strange things, but that's not my fault... Take a look at this. Have you ever seen it before?'

His hand dived into his pocket, and he threw the gold lighter on to the bed. Renée uttered a cry and shrank back from it as though it had been a scorpion.

'Go on! Look at it... It's a lighter... Touch it; take it in your hand. I tell you, it's only a lighter. It won't bite you... Well? Doesn't it remind you of anything?'

'No.'

'Not a visit to the Louvre?'

'No.'

'I picked it up near your body... It's true you couldn't remember my doing that.'

He said that in a slightly sneering tone and Renée's tears began flowing again.

'Go away,' she whimpered. 'Leave me alone.'

'Keep it,' went on Flavières. 'Keep it. It's yours.'

It lay there glittering between them like a sort of ominous challenge. Looking across it at Renée, Flavières saw a woman he was torturing needlessly. Needlessly? His blood was throbbing at his temples. He trailed over to the wash-basin and gulped down some tepid water that tasted of disinfectant. He had still a host of questions to ask her. They writhed in his brain like worms. But they must wait… He had put Madeleine to flight by his haste, his rough handling. He must coax her back little by little to the threshold of life. He would reconstitute her out of Renée's substance. Then… The moment would come when she would remember. He turned the key in the lock.

'I can't stay here,' said Renée.

'Where would you go to?'

'I don't know. Anywhere, so long as I get away.'

'I won't touch you, I promise… I'll never speak about the past again.'

He could hear her breathing rapidly. He knew, as he undressed, that she was following every movement.

'Take that lighter away,' she cried and her voice was full of horror.

'Really? Won't you keep it?'

'No. I only want to be left in peace. I had a bad enough time during the war. If I've now got to…'

She flicked away a tear from the corner of her eye, groped for her handkerchief. Flavières threw her his, but she pretended not to notice.

'Why are you angry?' he asked. 'I didn't mean to be nasty. Come on, let's make it up.'

He picked up his handkerchief, sat down on the bed, and wiped her eyes. A brusque tenderness made his movements awkward. Her tears flowed on steadily like blood from a wound that wouldn't heal.

'There's nothing to cry about,' he kept repeating. 'There's nothing to cry about.'

He pressed her head against his breast and rocked her gently.

'There are times,' he said softly, 'when I hardly know what I'm doing. I'm so tortured by memories... I don't suppose you could ever understand... If she had died peacefully in bed... of course I should have suffered... but I'd have got over it, perhaps even forgotten... The thing is... I may as well tell you now... She killed herself. She threw herself from the top of a tower. What she did it for, what she was trying to escape from... for five years I've been racking my brains for an answer to that question.'

A muffled sob was Renée's only answer.

'There! It's all over now. You see, I've told you the whole story... I need you, my little one. You must never leave me, for this time I should die. It's quite true... I'm still in love with her. I'm in love with you too. And it's one and the same love, a love such as no man has ever known before... It would be perfect if only you could just make that effort... if you could tell me what happened... *after that*.'

The head he was holding moved but he grasped it the more firmly.

'No. Let me go on... I'll tell you something, something which I've only realized myself in the last few days.'

He felt for the switch and turned off the light. He was in an uncomfortable position, but didn't think of changing it.

Pressed together, they drifted in the dusk, with vague forms floating around them. They were half-drowned beings seeking to come up into the lost light of day.

'I've always been afraid of dying,' Flavières went on in a voice that was now no more than a whisper. 'The death of other people upset me terribly because it foretold my own. And my own… no, I have never been able to resign myself to the idea… I came near to believing in the Christian God because of the promise of the resurrection… That body wrapped in a linen cloth, the great stone rolled to the door of the sepulchre, the soldiers watching… And then, the third day… When I was a boy, how I used to ponder over that third day… I went secretly up to an empty cave and shouted into it. The sound echoed under the ground, but no one rose from the dead… It was too early then… Now… now I believe my shout was answered… I want so desperately to believe it. If it were true… if you could only tell me… you… Ah! What a relief it would be… I would send the doctors about their business. You, you would teach me to…'

He looked down at the dim face whose orbits seemed empty. Only the forehead, cheeks, and chin were touched by a faint light. His heart was full of love; he gazed at her, waiting perhaps for some word from her. Another tram screeched round the bend, and the flashes from the contact flickered on the walls and ceiling. Her eyes, too, flashed for a moment with a weird green sparkle. He started.

'Shut your eyes,' he said. 'You must never look at me like that again.'

His right arm was completely numb. The whole of that side of him seemed to be dead. He thought of the moment when, in the Seine, dragged down by Madeleine's weight, he had had to

160

struggle for his own life as well as hers. He was being dragged down again now, but he no longer had the wish to struggle. He was tempted to yield, to abandon his role as guide and protector. After all, it was she who knew the secret…

Sleep was already clouding his thoughts. He tried once again to speak. He wanted to promise her something, but what it was was obscured by too many mists. He was vaguely aware that she moved, no doubt to undress. He tried to say to her:

'Stay with me, Madeleine.'

But his lips scarcely moved. He slept but without any real repose. Only towards dawn did his spirit seem to be at peace, and he was quite unconscious of her when she looked at him for a long time in the grey morning light, her eyes once again slowly filling with tears.

He woke up with a headache, feeling washed out. Sounds of splashing in the bathroom reassured him. When he got out of bed, he felt an absolute wreck.

'I shan't be a minute,' cried Renée.

His mind bereft of thought or any feeling of pleasure, he gazed absently at the blue sky over the roofs opposite. Another day! Life went on: another day as stupid as its predecessors! He dressed listlessly. As on every other morning, he was racked by the longing for a drink. He had a nip. That cleared his mind a bit, but only for him to find all his anxieties intact, all his questions neatly arranged side by side like the cutlery in a canteen. Renée emerged in a magnificent dressing-gown, bought the previous day.

'There you are. You can have the bathroom now.'

'No hurry… Did you sleep well?… I'm feeling rotten this morning. Did I talk in my sleep?'

'No.'

'I do sometimes. When I have nightmares. There's nothing in that: I've had them all my life.'

He yawned, then studied her. She didn't look any too good either, but now that she was thinner she troubled his spirit more than ever. She began doing her hair. Once again, Flavières couldn't restrain himself: he snatched the comb out of her hand.

'Here! Give that to me.'

He pulled a chair forward in front of the looking-glass.

'Sit down. I'll show you… Having your hair on your shoulders doesn't suit you a bit.'

He tried to pass it off lightly, but his hands trembled with impatience.

'As a matter of fact, what it really needs is a touch of henna. Some strands are lighter than others. It is neither one thing nor the other.'

Her lustrous hair crackled under the comb. It felt warm to his touch and smelt of burnt prairies, like the fumes of new wine. Flavières held his breath. Renée, her lips slightly retracted, showing her teeth, abandoned herself to the soothing, caressing movements of the comb. Soon he was forming a bun at the back of her neck—with much too many pins, of course, but he didn't pretend to be an expert. He only wanted to remodel the shape of her head, giving it the noble line, the serenity of a Leonardo. To put it differently, he was painting the portrait of the Madeleine he remembered. And he was succeeding! There was the fine fore-head now, the delicate ears revealed. Putting in the last pin, he straightened himself, and looked in the glass to survey his work.

Yes, it was good: There, within the frame of the mirror touched by a slanting ray of sunshine, there, clear and limpid as a water-colour, was the pale, mysterious face, withdrawn and thoughtful.

'Madeleine!'

He murmured the name, but she didn't even hear him. Was that really the reflection of a woman that he was staring at in the glass? Or was it some subjective vision like the things seen in a crystal? He crept round the chair to face her. No, he hadn't deceived himself. It was Madeleine as he had known her. For the slow rhythmic movements of the comb had plunged her into a sort of dream, a mood of grave meditation.

Realizing she was being scrutinized, she heaved a sigh, shook herself, made an effort to smile.

'If you'd gone on a little longer,' she said, 'I'd have fallen fast asleep.'

She looked casually into the glass.

'Not bad,' she commented. 'Yes, it's perhaps better like that. It's another matter whether it'll hold.'

She shook her head, and the pins began falling out. Another shake, and her hair fell down altogether. She burst out laughing. He laughed too, though, with him, it was rather the reaction from the intense fear which had gripped him.

'*Mon pauvre chéri*,' she said.

He went on laughing, holding his hands to his head, but he felt he couldn't remain in that room any longer. He found it suffocating. He needed the sunshine, the rumbling of the trams, the jostling of the crowd. He needed to forget as quickly as possible what he had seen. He dashed into the bathroom to get ready. His hands fumbled with the taps; when he brushed his teeth, he nearly dropped the tumbler.

'I'll go down ahead of you,' she suggested.

'No. Wait for me. You can wait a moment, can't you?'

His voice was so changed that she came to the bathroom door.

'What's the matter with you?'

'Nothing... What makes you think there is?'

He noticed she now had her hair arranged as usual, but couldn't make up his mind whether to be angry or relieved. He tied his tie anyhow, slipped on his jacket, and took her arm.

'You needn't think I'm lost,' she remarked jokingly.

But he couldn't bring himself to laugh now.

When they left the hotel, they didn't know what to do with themselves. Every prospect seemed equally boring. Flavières felt tired already. His headache was hammering at his skull. He had to sit down in a public garden, but they were no sooner installed than he said:

'I'm sorry. I'm afraid we'll have to go back... I'm not feeling well at all.'

She pursed her lips and avoided looking at him, but she obediently helped him back to the hotel. There she settled down to darn some stockings, while he tried to pull himself together. How long would she consent to remain shut up with him in that dreary room, as little homely as a waiting-room? He had no right to hold her against her will. He guessed he had not succeeded in reassuring her—not altogether. At lunchtime he tried to get up, but sank back on to the bed again, feeling giddy.

'Would you like me to put a cold compress on your forehead?'

'No... no... It'll pass off... Go and have lunch.'

'Really?'

'Yes. I mean it. I'll be all right.'

Yet, when she shut the door behind her, his face was at once distorted by intense anxiety. It was silly, he knew. All her things were there in the wardrobe. She couldn't run off, she couldn't disappear…

'But she might die,' he thought.

That idea was no less silly. He put both hands to his forehead, trying to banish it. The time passed. Grain by grain he could hear it drop, as through an hour-glass. The waiters were slow, he knew. All the same, she could have skipped a course or two. No doubt she was, on the contrary, taking advantage of being alone to guzzle, choosing all the things she had usually to go without because he didn't like to see her eating them. The animal side of her—how he hated it!… Already in the little café at Courbevoie, when she had emerged from the kitchen dressed like a skivvy, how he had suffered!

She'd been gone an hour now. One might think she was starving! By the end of an hour and a quarter, worry and anger were added to his headache. Tears of impotent rage welled up into his eyes. When she came back at last, he looked at her balefully.

'An hour and twenty minutes to swallow down a wretched bit of steak!'

She laughed, sat down on the bed, and took his hand.

'There were snails,' she said. 'I thought the menu was never coming to an end. What about you?'

'Me! As though—'

'Now, now! Don't be childish.'

He clung to her cool hand, and gradually calmed down. Presently he dozed off, still clinging to it as though it was some precious toy. When he woke up a little after four, he felt a little better and wanted to go out.

'But not far. Tomorrow I'll go and see a doctor.'

They went down. On the pavement, Flavières pretended to have forgotten something.

'Wait a moment, will you? I've just got to put through a telephone call.'

Dashing into the bar, he ordered a whisky.

'As quick as you can.'

He was trembling with impatience, like a traveller who fears to miss his train. Perhaps she wouldn't wait… Perhaps she would have already turned the corner. Perhaps… He took a long draught, relishing the warmth spreading through his chest. His eyes fell on a menu propped up on the bar.

'Is that the menu for lunch?'

'Yes, Monsieur.'

'I don't see any mention of snails.'

'There weren't any snails.'

Deep in thought, Flavières finished his drink and wiped his mouth.

'Put it down on the bill,' he said, and hurried out to join her.

He was pleasant; he talked a lot; he could be quite brilliant when he took the trouble. In the evening he took her to a smart restaurant down by the Old Port. Yes, he was amiable, but could she see what was behind it? Probably not. His manner was too unaccountable, their relations too artificial, for her to notice.

They got back late and stayed late in bed next morning. When lunchtime approached, he again complained of a headache.

'You see what it does to you to keep late hours,' she said.

'It doesn't matter. I'm only sorry on your account. You'll have to have lunch alone again today.'

'I shan't be long this time.'

'Don't hurry.'

Flavières listened to her retreating steps, then sneaked down after her. A glance round the hall, another round the dining-room. No sign of her. Going out he spotted her at once some distance down the street.

'Here we are!' he said to himself. 'It's beginning all over again.'

She was wearing the grey suit. Around her danced the shadows of the lime trees. She walked quickly, looking at the pavement, taking no notice of anything. As before, there were plenty of officers about. On the placards, the news too was much the same: *Bombardements... Défaite Imminente...* She turned down a side street, and Flavières drew closer. It was a narrow street with shops on either side. Mostly books and antiques. Hadn't he seen it before? Not it, but another like it, the Rue des Saints-Pères. Renée crossed over to the other side and dived into a little hotel. Flavières couldn't bring himself to follow. A superstitious fear rooted him to the pavement, staring at the marble plaque on which was written *Central Hôtel* and at the notice hanging on the handle of the door which said: *Complet.*

All the same he had to go. His legs felt weak, but he dragged himself across the road and opened the door through which she had disappeared. His eyes took in the poky hall and lighted on the board behind the desk, from which, no doubt, she had just taken her key.

'Yes?' asked the man at the desk.

'That lady?... The lady in grey... Who is she?'

'The one that just came in?'

'Yes. What's her name?'

'Pauline Lagerlac,' answered the man with a horrible Marseilles accent.

FIVE

When Renée got back to the hotel, Flavières was lying down.

'How do you feel?' she asked.

'A bit better. I think I'll get up.'

'Why are you looking at me like that?'

'Like what?'

He sat up, trying to smile.

'You certainly gave me a queer look,' she insisted. 'Have I done anything to upset you?'

'No… Really not.'

He got up, combed his hair, and brushed his jacket. In this small room they were absolutely on top of each other all the time. He couldn't bring himself to speak, nor could he make up his mind to remain silent. What he really wanted was to be alone, alone with the terrible mystery.

'I've got to go out again,' said Renée. 'I've a few things to do.'

'What things?'

'First of all I must get my hair washed, and I must buy a pair of stockings.'

To get her hair washed, to buy a pair of stockings—that sounded homely and comforting. In any case she was looking at him now with such engaging frankness that it was impossible to suspect her of lying.

'May I?' she asked.

He made a gesture of tenderness, but his hand faltered like a blind man's.

'You're not a prisoner,' he murmured. 'You know very well which of us is in captivity here.'

Another silence. She powdered her nose in front of the looking-glass, Flavières standing behind her.

'You get on my nerves, *chéri*,' she remarked.

Her hair tumbled playfully over her ears. He gazed at a tiny vein on her temple through which he could almost feel the blood coursing. Yes, this body was full of vitality, and, if his eyes were more penetrating, he would be able to see it, like an aura. He touched her neck; the flesh was smooth and warm. Quickly he withdrew his hand.

'Really, what is the matter with you?' she said, adding a touch of red to her lips.

He sighed. Renée… Madeleine… Pauline… What was the good of asking her the same eternal questions?

'Run along,' he said gently. 'Be as quick as you can.'

He handed her her gloves, her bag.

'I'll be waiting for you downstairs… You will come back, won't you?'

'Don't be silly! What an idea!'

He forced himself to smile. He was terribly unhappy. He had all the air of a defeated man, and he was conscious of her sudden pity. Yes, she was hesitating to go, like someone ashamed of leaving the bedside of a condemned man. She loved him, yes; but in the expression on her face he could see at the same time great tenderness and great cruelty. She took a step towards him, lifted her head, and kissed him on the lips. What did she mean? Was she saying good-bye to him?… He gently stroked her cheek.

'Forgive me… little Eurydice!'

She seemed to turn a little paler beneath her make-up. She blinked rapidly.

'Be reasonable, *mon chéri*. Have a good rest. Stop teasing your poor brain for a little while.'

She paused at the door and waved to him. Then she was gone. He stayed where he was, gazing at the handle, but it didn't turn. Would it ever?… Yes. She would come back… But when? He felt like rushing out into the corridor and shouting after her:

'Madeleine! Madeleine!'

But it was true what he had said just now: it was he who was the prisoner. What could he hope for? To keep her with him in that room? To stand guard over her night and day? Even that would never give him access to what was hidden in the depths of her memory. The real Madeleine was free, but she lived elsewhere. This replica of her she had vouchsafed him was merely a sop. A temporary one at that. Their separation sooner or later was inevitable. For their love was something monstrous, foredoomed to death… To death!

Flavières gave a savage kick to the chair in front of the dressing-table. Rubbish! What about that hotel in which she had already taken a room? Nothing mysterious about that. It pointed to one thing and one thing only—flight. After Gévigne there had been Almaryan, with perhaps others in between. Then Flavières—with others after… Was he jealous? And, if so, of whom? Madeleine! Did that make any sense?

He lit a cigarette with the gold lighter and went down to the bar. He wasn't hungry. He didn't even want a drink, but ordered a cognac just to give himself the right to occupy one of the easy chairs. The place was practically dead at that hour.

A single light lit up the many-coloured bottles; the barman was reading the paper. Leaning back in his chair, with his glass in the hollow of his hand, Flavières could at last shut his eyes. And the first image that rose to his mind was Gévigne's. He had treated Gévigne disgracefully. It served him right, no doubt, if he was now in the same position himself. In a sense he had become Gévigne. It was his turn now to live with a strange elusive woman. And if, like him, he had had an old friend to turn to, wouldn't he have done so? Of course; and he would have asked him to keep an eye on Renée; for he had reached that point now... He could see Gévigne sitting in his office; he could hear him saying:

'She's queer... I'm worried about her.'

He opened his eyes.

'Waiter! Bring me another.'

Fortunately Gévigne had never suspected the truth. If he had... what would he have done? The same as Flavières had, no doubt: taken to drink. Or would he have put a bullet through his head? For there are some truths which you can't dwell on without feeling that giddy nausea of the soul which is a hundred times worse than anything that can happen to the body... And he, Flavières, had been chosen from amongst all mankind to bear the burden of this secret. A secret which brought no joy, which merely made it twice as hard to live.

He felt perfectly calm now and quite extraordinarily clear-headed. He could even delve back into the past without flinching, seeing the crumpled body at the foot of the tower, the blood on the stones. Later, Gévigne had wept over the body of his wife, which the old woman had laid out. Detectives had examined it too and asked all sorts of questions. That didn't bother him: he was as indifferent as the Roman soldiers playing dice at the foot of the cross. The ordeal started when he thought of Pauline Lagerlac's suicide, when he thought of Madeleine's first words to him: 'It doesn't hurt', and above all when he conjured up the scene in the church and her serene resolve… Life had become too much of a strain to her and she was going quite simply to walk out of it… But was Renée's life any less of a strain? Probably not. In that case… With that thought, Flavières' head began to swim, and he was assailed by a horrible feeling of emptiness, an emptiness like space itself, limitless, unceasing, and without reprieve.

'Waiter.'

This time he was genuinely thirsty. He gazed despairingly at the sombre upholstery around him and the row of bottles behind the bar. Was he still in the land of the living himself? Yes. His forehead was perspiring, his hands burning. Yes, he was alive and his mind was imbued with a frightening acuity. He was well aware, with a painful intensity even, of the absurdity of the situation. He would now no longer be able to sleep with Renée, no longer be able even to speak to her. She was too *different*. A barrier had been raised between them by that visit of hers to the little hotel. She would inevitably fall into the arms of some other man, who would be able to love her in ignorance. That was what she wanted, no doubt; Gévigne had almost found out, and she had killed herself. Now…

He let his glass slip out of his hand and the brandy spilt all over his knee. He wiped it with his handkerchief. With a shame-faced look at the barman, still deep in his newspaper, he picked up the sticky glass. He was furious with himself for not having guessed sooner. Now she was obviously running away. No doubt she had already transported some of her things to the little hotel, taking a few at a time… She might well be planning the next hop, buying a ticket for Africa or America… And that, for him, would be worse than death.

He stood up, tottered, grasped the back of the chair. The barman looked up.

'Are you feeling queer, Monsieur?'

He came round and took Flavières' arm.

'Let go. I'm all right.'

Flavières held on to the chromium rod that ran along the front of the bar, staring stupidly at the white jacket of the barman at his side.

'Really. I'm better now, thanks.'

'What about a whisky to put you right?'

'Yes… Thanks… A whisky.'

He gulped it down. He was disgusted with himself for being so weak, but he knew the whisky would soon pull him together. He would find a way to stop Madeleine going. As a matter of fact it was entirely his fault if she was planning to, with his ceaseless allusions and insinuations. He had, little by little, been recreating Madeleine, without suspecting that, by doing so, he was preparing her departure. How could he undo that work? How could he convince her that they could go on living as before? He couldn't: it was too late.

He looked at the clock. Half past four.

'Put it down on my bill.'

He tried letting go of the chromium rod. He staggered slightly, then found his feet. He went out into the hall and beckoned the Buttons.

'Is there a ladies' hairdresser's near here?… A smart one, of course.'

'*Chez Maryse*… That's the nearest.'

'How far?'

'Barely five minutes' walk. You go along the boulevard, then take the third turning on the right. You'll find it between a café and a florist's. You can't miss it.'

'Thank you.'

Flavières went out looking dazed. He'd made a mistake not having any lunch. The glitter of the sun on the tramlines was almost unbearable. Life flowed through the streets like a river in spate and Flavières had sometimes to hug the walls, not to be swept along by it. He found the hairdresser's without difficulty and peered in through the window like a beggar. There she was, with a complicated apparatus over her head. Yes, it was Renée. She was there. A respite had been granted them.

'*Merci!*' he muttered. '*Merci!*'

Then he passed on and went into the café next door.

'A glass of beer and a sandwich, please.'

From now on he was going to take care. Of his health, too, for he needed all his energies. He would have to be strong to prevent her going. He would have to be prudent to allay her misgivings. He must avoid any allusion to the past. He must renounce the attempt to make her confess.

He sighed and gave up trying to finish his sandwich. The beer disgusted him. His mouth was foul from too much smoking. He fidgeted in his seat, trying to find a comfortable position. He had a view of the pavement in front of the hairdresser's, so she couldn't give him the slip. She'd go straight back to the hotel, no doubt. How were they then to get through the long evening? Should he ask her forgiveness, beg her to forget their quarrels?... Gazing out of the window, he had the impression he was sitting for a very difficult exam: questions were being fired at him and he couldn't find the answers. He understood himself well enough to know he would never give up trying to find out. What he loved in her was, not that she was Madeleine, but that she was alive. And it was just that, her bubbling vitality, that she declined to share with him. She was too rich, he too poor. All right; but he would never accept being shut out from the secret... Where was he getting to now?

The time passed slowly. From a distance the proprietor of the café watched the peculiar customer who muttered to himself and who seemed unable to take his eyes off the street. And Flavières' sombre meditations went on. There was no way out, at least no good one. Madeleine was bound to leave him. He had no means of preventing her. The first suitable opportunity, and it would be all over. He would no longer be able to afford a headache and stay in bed for half a day... Perhaps it was already too late. Perhaps, instead of going back to the hotel, she would go to the station or to some ship on the point of sailing. Leaving him with nothing to do but die.

Suddenly Madeleine came out. She appeared as suddenly as if she had risen from the pavement. She was bare-headed. Her hair, done in a bun at the back, was lightly tinted with henna.

Flavières dashed out. She walked in front of him with a leisurely step, her black bag under her arm. She wore the grey suit he had bought her. She was just as he had conjured her up in his dreams. He gained on her a little. It was all exactly like that day on the banks of the Seine, even to the point of his catching a whiff of her perfume, which smelt of the autumn, of the earth, of dead leaves. Flavières walked like a sleep-walker. One hand was pressed to his heart; his mouth was open. It was altogether too much for him. He stumbled; he brushed past people, who stared at him in astonishment. Was he going to fall down? Or burst into tears?

She walked down, rather aimlessly to all appearances, towards the ruins of the Old Port. She certainly wasn't making for the hotel. How right he had been to keep her under observation. Was she going to meet someone? Or just taking a walk—enjoying a last half-hour of peace before plunging back into the torments of a relationship that had become impossible? Or was she already elsewhere, a stranger in a strange town?

The growl of bulldozers could be heard behind blackened mutilated walls, plastered with posters. Children played among the ruins. With her easy, swinging walk, Madeleine reached the Quai des Beiges. She stopped for a moment to look at the wreckage of the transporter-bridge. The grey water reflected the yellow hulls of sailing-boats, moored up side by side and sleeping peacefully. A boy standing astride in the stern-sheets of a boat was sculling with an oar over the transom. Here and there a disused lighter was rotting against the wall. This was Marseilles, but it was also Courbevoie. The past merged into the incomprehensible present. Flavières had the feeling he had stepped out of time altogether. And those ripples on which bits of wood and orange peel bobbed up and down—perhaps they didn't really exist at all. Nor Madeleine either… All the same there was that scent which the smells of the port couldn't altogether obliterate.

Madeleine followed the quays towards the tidal basins. Was she going to board a liner? Or had she merely come to gaze at the ships, dreaming of some country she hankered after? Men of nondescript race, dressed in American jumpers and trousers with enormous pockets, wandered casually about the quays and warehouses, but Madeleine seemed not to notice anyone. She studied the water shimmering here and there with a film of oil, then, lifting her head, looked through the forests of masts and spars over to the black walls of Fort Saint-Jean. Here and there a sentry, his rifle at the slope, stood guard over a dump of military stores. Tired as he was, Flavières didn't even think of stopping. He was waiting for the inevitable.

It was on the Quai de la Joliette that the inevitable happened. There, Madeleine sat down at the one and only table in front of a sort of café. Inevitable, too, were the barrels for him to hide behind. And, as the lights in the ships and warehouses went on one by one, she once again began writing. Her pen moved quickly. This time, it was to him that she was writing. She was trying gently to explain things to him as formerly she had to Gévigne. And Flavières was sick with fear and misery. Now she folded the letter, licked the flap of the envelope, left some money on the table, and walked away.

Flavières followed with horror in his heart. Was the other thing inevitable too? Was she going to... No. Not here at any rate. He felt sure she would seek a more deserted spot. Anyhow, she was walking between the railway lines, some distance from the edge of the quay, so there was no immediate danger... One behind the other they passed the bows of huge ships whose hawsepipes watched them like eyes. High up above them, a sailor leant over the side-rails and flicked the ash off his cigarette. Huge hawsers looped down in all directions from the fairleads. Insects buzzed in the halos round the lights on the quay. Madeleine was hurrying now, one hand holding her skirt which was flying about in the wind. She approached the edge, ducked under a hawser. Here there was no one about. At the bottom of some steps, two dinghies were rubbing against each other. Flavières crept up to her on tip-toe. As soon as he was within reach of her, he seized her by the shoulders and pulled her back. She uttered a cry and struggled.

'It's me,' he said. 'Give me that letter.'

They each tugged at her bag which suddenly flew open. The letter fell to the ground and was instantly caught by the wind. Flavières tried to put his foot on it, but was a second too late. A stronger gust took it over the edge of the quay, and a moment later it was floating, out of reach in the water. Flavières still held her fast.

'Look what you've done!'

'Let me go.'

He stuffed her bag in his pocket and dragged her away.

'I've been following you all the way from the hairdresser's. What made you come here? And what was in that letter? Were you saying good-bye? Answer me.'

'Yes.'

He shook her.

'And then… What were you intending to do?'

'Go away… Tomorrow, perhaps… I can't stand this any longer.'

'And what about me?'

He felt empty and shrivelled up. His shoulders drooped with fatigue.

'Come on. Let's get back.'

They dived through narrow slummy streets, peopled by dubious types. But Flavières had no fear of them, for the simple reason he was unconscious of them. His fingers firmly gripped her elbow. He had the impression he had brought her back from some distant country, from the pastures of the dead.

'Now,' he said, 'I've a right to know. You're Madeleine, aren't you?'

'No.'

'Then who are you?'

'Renée Sourange.'

'It's not true.'

'It is.'

He looked up at the thin band of sky between the tall blind houses. He wanted to hit her, even to kill her.

'You are Madeleine,' he continued angrily. 'The proof is that when you went to the little hotel you gave your name as Pauline Lagerlac.'

'That was just to throw you off the scent, when you tried to find me.'

'To throw me off the scent?'

'Yes... Since you're so determined that I'm this Pauline... I was pretty sure you'd make enquiries and fetch up there sooner or later... I wanted you to conserve the memory... of the other... and forget Renée Sourange.'

'And why have you done your hair like that and tinted it with henna?'

'Same idea. To wipe Renée Sourange off the slate. So that you're left with nothing but your Madeleine.'

'It's you I want to keep.'

In despair, he squeezed her arm. In the murky twilight he could now identify her with absolute certainty, by her step, her scent, and the hundred and one other details that love can interpret so unerringly. Vague snatches of music, an accordion, a mandolin, came to them from somewhere or other. Behind them, an occasional blast of a siren sounded like some wild nocturnal beast.

'What made you want to run away?' he asked. 'Weren't you happy with me?'

'No.'

'Because of all those questions?'

'Yes… That… and other things.'

'And if I promised to drop the subject, never to pester you with questions again?'

'Poor dear! As though you could keep such a promise!'

'Listen… It's really very simple: confess that you're Madeleine and we'll never refer to it again… We'll go right away from here and start all over afresh. We could have a wonderful life together.'

'I'm not Madeleine.'

Again! This incredible obstinacy!

'You're so completely Madeleine that you've even got back that way of looking at nothing, as though you had floated off into another world.'

'I've got worries enough.'

'What worries?'

'Worries of my own that I can't share with anybody.'

He was aware she was crying. They were coming to a well-lit boulevard. There they would get a foothold again in the world of the living. Flavières took out his handkerchief.

'Here. Let me have a go at that face.'

He wiped her cheeks tenderly and kissed her eyes. He took her by the hand.

'Come on. Don't be afraid.'

They turned into the boulevard, jostled with the crowd. Bands were playing in the big cafés. Jeeps dashed past at full speed manned by soldiers in white helmets. On the kerb were hawkers, men selling monkey-nuts; spivs asked for a light, then offered packets of *Lucky Strike*. Whenever Flavières looked at Madeleine, she turned her head away. She was unbending, her lips set resentfully. But Flavières was too unhappy himself to have much pity for her.

'Let me go,' she said. 'I want to buy some aspirin. It's my turn to have a headache now.'

'First of all admit that you're Madeleine.'

She shrugged her shoulders and they went on as before. Just like two lovers. Yet he held her arm more like a policeman who's made his catch and isn't taking any risks.

At the hotel, they went straight into the dining-room. Flavières simply couldn't take his eyes off her. Under the bright lights, with her hair done like that, she looked exactly as she had the first time he had seen her, at the *Théâtre Marigny*. He stretched his hand across the table and squeezed her fingers.

'Don't you want to say anything?' he asked.

She looked down. She was pale as death. The head waiter came up and took their order.

'And what wine would you like?'

'*Moulin-à-Vent*.'

He felt disembodied, as though Madeleine's presence had deprived him of reality, of all substance. As he looked at her he thought sometimes:

'It's impossible!'

And sometimes:

'I must be asleep.'

She hardly ate anything. Several times she began to slip into one of those reveries which he had known so well of old. He drank the whole of the bottle, deliberately, one might almost say methodically. He felt Madeleine's hostility between them like a steel partition.

'Come on,' he said at last. 'I can see you're at the end of your tether... Do say something, Madeleine.'

She got up immediately.

'I'll catch you up,' he said.

And while she fetched the key of their room, he had just time to gulp down a glass of whisky at the bar. He joined her at the lift.

The gate was shut and up they went. Flavières put his arm round Madeleine's shoulders. He leant over, as though to kiss her, but merely whispered in her ear:

'Confess, *chérie*.'

She leant heavily against the mahogany wall of the lift.

'All right,' she said. 'I am Madeleine.'

SIX

Automatically he turned the key in the lock. This confession he had waited for for so long, far from making things clearer, had plunged him back into the fogs. For one thing, was it really a confession at all? She had made it with such utter lassitude! Perhaps she had said the words merely to please him, to obtain a truce. Leaning with his back against the door, he said:

'How can I believe you?'

'Do you want proofs?'

'No, but…'

He was bewildered. God! How tired he was!

'Switch off the light,' she pleaded.

Through the slatted shutters, the street lamps threw bars of light and shade across the ceiling. Bars! Yes, the cage he had closed upon them. Flavières threw himself down on the bed.

'Why didn't you tell me the truth at once? What were you frightened of?'

He couldn't see Madeleine, but he could hear her moving over by the bathroom.

'Answer me. What were you frightened of?'

She still said nothing, and he went on:

'You recognized me the moment you saw me at the *Waldorf*, didn't you?'

'Yes. Immediately.'

'Then you should have confided in me at once. All this play-acting! What possessed you to behave so stupidly!'

He brought his fist down so violently on the bed that the springs answered with a metallic twang.

'What a farce!… Do you think that was worthy of us?… And that letter!… Instead of telling me frankly to my face what happened to you…'

She came and sat beside him, feeling for his hand in the darkness.

'I didn't want you ever to know.'

'But I've known all along…'

'Listen… Let me explain… Though it's terribly difficult.'

Her hand was burning. Flavières didn't move. All his muscles were contracted. At last he was going to hear the secret—and how he dreaded it!

'The woman you knew in Paris,' she began, 'the one you saw in the theatre with your friend Gévigne, the one you followed, the one you fished out of the water—that woman never died. Do you understand? I never died!'

Flavières smiled.

'Of course not,' he said. 'You just became Renée.'

'No, *mon chéri*, no… If only that could be true!… I didn't become Renée: I always was Renée. That's my real name, Renée Sourange. And it's me, Renée Sourange, that you've been in love with all along.'

'What do you mean?'

'You never knew Madeleine Gévigne. I impersonated her. I was Gévigne's accomplice… Forgive me if you can. You don't know how much I've suffered for it.'

Flavières seized her wrist roughly.

'Are you trying to tell me that the body at the foot of the church tower…'

'Yes. It was Madame Gévigne. Her husband had just killed her… Madeleine Gévigne was the one who died, while I remained alive… There you are! That's the truth.'

'It's not. I refuse to believe it. It's easy to say things like that now, when Gévigne's no longer here to contradict you. Poor Gévigne. So you were his mistress—that's what you're telling me, is it? And you concocted that plot between you, to get rid of his lawful wife. But why?'

'She had the money… We were intending to go abroad.'

'Splendid! And why should Gévigne come to me and ask me to keep his wife under observation?'

'Don't get excited, *chéri*.'

'I'm not getting excited. I've never been calmer in my life. Come on, tell me.'

'To divert suspicion. You see, his wife had no reason to commit suicide. He needed someone who could come forward and say that Madame Gévigne had strange ideas, that she was convinced she had lived before, that death seemed to her of no importance, almost a game; someone who would be believed without question when he said he had already witnessed one attempt of hers to take her life… You're a lawyer… and then… he had known you so well… he knew you'd swallow the story without a murmur.'

'Ah! So he took me for a fool, or someone with a screw loose, did he!… What a pretty plan! So it was you at the theatre, you at the cemetery, you whose photograph was on his desk when I went to see him…'

'Yes.'

'And now you'll be telling me Pauline Lagerlac never existed.'

'Oh yes, she did.'

'Ah! So that's one thing you can't deny.'

'Please! Do try to understand,' she sighed.

'I understand perfectly,' he snarled. 'I understand everything. And I can see very well that Pauline Lagerlac's a bit of a nuisance. She rather spoils the story.'

'I wish it was a story,' she murmured. 'Pauline Lagerlac really was Madeleine Gévigne's great-grandmother. In fact it was she who gave your friend the idea—the obsession with a strange ancestor, the pilgrimage to her tomb and to the house in the Rue des Saints-Pères in which Pauline had lived, the faked attempt at suicide, since Pauline had drowned herself…'

'Did you say faked?'

'Yes. To pave the way to… to the other one. If you hadn't dragged me out, I'd have been all right. I'm a good swimmer.'

Flavières stowed his hands away in his pockets for fear of hitting her.

'A very clever man, your Gévigne!' he sneered. 'He seems to have thought of everything. And when he suggested I should go to his house to meet you, I suppose he knew I should refuse?'

'He was right. You did refuse. And afterwards I told you never to ring me up at the Avenue Kléber.'

'That's enough… Assuming for a moment… But what about the church tower? How could he know we'd go there?… I suppose you'll say that you were driving, that that isolated village had already been chosen and every detail worked out, right down to the exact time, that he'd only got to ask his wife to come out with him, only got to ask her to wear such and such a dress, to please him… All the same, in spite of all you may say, I don't believe you. Do you hear? I don't believe you... Gévigne wasn't a criminal.'

'I'm afraid he was. Admittedly there were things to be said on his side. He'd married badly. Madeleine really was... a bit ill, let us call it. He had taken her to one doctor after another, but they could never make out quite what was wrong.'

'Of course! And of course it's easy to think up explanations afterwards. The tower—no difficulty about that. Gévigne was there, up at the top, waiting for you, having already killed his wife and disfigured her sufficiently to make the face unrecognizable. He knew I had no head for heights and would never get past that door if it meant climbing out on to the cornice. Then, when you joined him, he had only to chuck the body overboard while you screamed. And then you peeped out and watched me go up to the body, which was dressed exactly as you were, the hair done the same way and tinged with henna... Oh yes, I can invent explanations too!... When you saw me go off...'

He was panting. The story was drilling its way into his brain, gaining plausibility from a hundred details that fitted in. He went on, muttering to himself:

'I ought to have raised the alarm, called in the police. Gévigne counted on that, counted on my making a statement describing the suicide. But I didn't. I didn't want once again to advertise my physical weakness. That's where Gévigne slipped up. He didn't foresee my silence, the silence of a man who has already allowed another to die in his place for the same reason...'

Flavières was quite right there: the plan had gone wrong. He recalled his visit to the flat in the Avenue Kléber, Gévigne's obvious terror (for of course he too was condemned to silence) and those words of his over the telephone the next morning: '*I was right, you know. She's killed herself… The police have started an enquiry… All the same, I'd have liked you to be with me…*'

A last desperate attempt to get Flavières to play his part. And his lie about the face not being disfigured. He knew Flavières hadn't been able to look at it. Since those horrible precautions had been superfluous, better to say nothing about them!… Yes, his silence had ruined the plan, and the police had started poking their noses into Gévigne's matrimonial affairs. The motive was plain as a pikestaff: she held the purse-strings… and he couldn't possibly produce an alibi, since he'd been in the church tower at the time… Some peasants had come forward to say they had seen a couple in a car. The Talbot with Gévigne and his wife: that was obvious now… And then Gévigne had been killed.

Renée was quietly crying, her head buried in the pillow. And Flavières suddenly realized that this was the end of everything. With his eyes open he had been living through a nightmare… So this woman who shared his room was Renée… Perhaps she had lived in the same building as Gévigne, and that was how he had got to know her… Weakly, she had agreed to play her part in the plot, and now, years later, out of weakness again, out of a sort of fatalism, she had consented to have an affair with the poor little lawyer who had been their dupe. No… No… He would never admit it. She had merely trumped up this story to get rid of him, because she didn't love him… For she had never loved him, neither in the old days nor…

'Madeleine,' he murmured beseechingly.

She dried her eyes, pushed back her hair.

'I'm not Madeleine,' she said.

And then, with his teeth clenched, he seized her by the throat with both hands.

'You're lying,' he groaned. 'You've never stopped lying... But can't you see that I love you, that I've always loved you—right from the start—because of Pauline, because of the cemetery, because of your dreamy eyes... A love like a marvellous tapestry—on one side it told a wonderful legend, on the other... I don't know... I don't want to know... But when I first put my arm round you I knew you were to be the only woman in my life... Madeleine... And our drives in the country together—don't you remember them? And the flowers, the Louvre, the lost country... Madeleine! I beg you—tell me the truth.'

She no longer moved. Painfully Flavières removed his fingers from her neck, and with a trembling hand switched on the light. Then he uttered a cry which brought people running out of their rooms into the corridor.

Flavières no longer wept. He looked at the bed. Even without the handcuffs, he would have kept his hands folded. The detective had just finished reading Dr. Ballard's letter to his colleague at Nice.

'Take him away,' he said.

The room was full of people, but no one made a sound.

'May I kiss her?' asked Flavières.

The detective shrugged his shoulders. Flavières went up to the bed. The dead girl looked so slim lying there, and written on her face was an immense peace. Flavières bent over and kissed her forehead.

'I shall wait for you,' he said.

—

Did you know?

Pierre Boileau and Thomas Narcejac met at an awards dinner. Narcejac was receiving the 1948 *Prix du roman d'aventures*, which is awarded for the best detective novel of the year in France, and which Boileau had already won ten years earlier. They got talking, and several years later, their first collaboration was published.

They wanted to try and develop a new type of crime fiction. They were tired of British who-dunnits and hardboiled American private eyes—they wanted to create a new style of mystery with the victim at its centre, albeit a victim who might not know they are a victim, and might even be a murderer! They went on to form an extraordinarily successful partnership, with Boileau supplying the fiendish, almost fantastical plots, and Narcejac the crucial characterization. As Boileau himself said, Narcejac "humanizes the most extraordinary situations… He turns a witch or a ghost into someone you might meet on the Metro". And, much like Hitchcock's bomb that must never explode, Boileau-Narcejac had one golden rule: the protagonist can never wake up from their nightmare.

Their first collaboration, *She Who Was No More*, appeared in 1952 and, so the story goes, Alfred Hitchcock was desperate to acquire the film rights. He was beaten to it by Henri-Georges Clouzot but moved heaven and earth to get the rights to *Vertigo* when it was published in 1954. Little did he know that Boileau-Narcejac had actually written it with him in mind!

So, where do you go from here?

If you enjoyed *Vertigo*'s hallucinatory plot and relentless tension, then you should take a look at **She Who Was No More**—Boileau-Narcejac's first book, and a classic thriller in the same mind-bending vein as *Vertigo*.

If you feel like something a little different, why not get hold of a copy of Soji Shimada's **The Tokyo Zodiac Murders**, the strangely brilliant, and utterly gruesome, locked-room puzzle that kicked off the Japanese *honkaku* "logic mystery" tradition?

AVAILABLE AND COMING SOON
FROM PUSHKIN VERTIGO

Augusto De Angelis

The Murdered Banker
The Mystery of the Three Orchids
The Hotel of the Three Roses

Piero Chiara

The Disappearance of Signora Giulia

Boileau-Narcejac

Vertigo
She Who Was No More

Alexander Lernet-Holenia

I Was Jack Mortimer

Leo Perutz

Master of the Day of Judgment
Little Apple
St Peter's Snow

Soji Shimada

The Tokyo Zodiac Murders
